When your life is a mess, and you are surrounded by enemies, how do you combat the overwhelming odds against you? Alice and Kathy must face down more than health concerns; life concerns and a litany of grievances are stacked against them.

A K'Anne Meinel novel

Also by K'Anne Meinel:

Novels in Paperback:

SHIPS *CompanionSHIP, FriendSHIP, RelationSHIP*
Long Distance Romance
Children of Another Mother
Erotica
The Claim
Bikini's Are Dangerous
The Complete Series
Germanic
Malice Masterpieces 1
The First Five Books
Represented
Timed Romance
Malice Masterpieces 2
Books Six through Ten
The Journey Home
Out at the Inn
Shorts
Anthology Volume 1
Lawyered
Malice Masterpieces 3
Books Eleven through Fifteen
Blown Away
Blown Away
The Alternate Cover

Small Town Angel
Pirated Love
Doctored
Veil of Silence
Malice Masterpieces 4
Books Sixteen through Twenty
The Outsider
Pirated Heart
Recombinant Love
Survivors
Inn the Dog House
Flight
An Island Between Us
Malice Masterpieces 5
Books Twenty-One through Twenty-Five
Malice Masterpieces 6
Books Twenty-Six through Thirty
Beauty and the Beast

Vetted Series:
Vetted
Cavalcade (Prequel)
Pioneering (Prequel)
Vetted Further
Vetted Again

Novellas in Paperback:

Sapphic Surfer
Sapphic Cowgirl
Sapphic Cowboi
Sayyida
The Northwood Lodge

The Malice Series:
Mysterious Malice (Book 1)
Meticulous Malice (Book 2)
Mistaken Malice (Book 3)
Malicious Malice (Book 4)
Masterful Malice (Book 5)
Matrimonial Malice (Book 6)
Mourning Malice (Book 7)
Murderous Malice (Book 8)
Mental Malice (Book 9)
Menacing Malice (Book 10)
Minor Malice (Book 11)
Morally Malice (Book 12)
Morose Malice (Book 13)
Melancholy Malice (Book 14)

Mad Malice (Book 15)
Macabre Malice (Book 16)
Marinating Malice (Book 17)
Macerating Malice (Book 18)
Minacious Malice (Book 19)
Meddlesome Malice (Book 20)
Meandering Malice (Book 21)
Maniacal Malice (Book 22)
Monitoring Malice (Book 23)
Marked Malice (Book 24)
Mandating Malice (Book 25)
Methodical Malice (Book 26)
Malevolent Malice (Book 27)
Militarial Malice (Book 28)
Machiavellian Malice (Book 29)
Malefic Malice (Book 30)

Religious Experience
Lied

All Novels and Novellas in paperback are also available as e-books.

A Woman Down Under Series:
Shanghaied (Prequel)
Outback Born
Outback Bred
Outback Heritage
Outback Native
Outback Splendor
Outback Yearnings (Prequel)
Outback Escape

Pocket Paperbacks:

Mysterious Malice (Book 1)
Sapphic Surfer
Sapphic Cowgirl
Meticulous Malice (Book 2)
Mistaken Malice (Book 3)
Malicious Malice (Book 4)
Masterful Malice (Book 5)
Matrimonial Malice (Book 6)
Mourning Malice (Book 7)
Murderous Malice (Book 8)
Mental Malice (Book 9)
Menacing Malice (Book 10)
Minor Malice (Book 11)
Morally Malice (Book 12)
Morose Malice (Book 13)
Melancholy Malice (Book 14)
Mad Malice (Book 15)
Macabre Malice (Book 16)
Marinating Malice (Book 17)

In E-Book Format:
Short Stories

Fantasy
Wet & Wet Again
Family Night
Quickie ~ Against the Car
Quickie ~ Against the Wall
Quickie ~ Over the Couch
Mile High Club
Quickie ~ Under the Pier
Heel or Heal
Kiss
Family Night 2
Beach Dreams
Internet Dreamers
Snoggered
On the Parkway
Stable Affair
Kept
Stolen
Agitated
Love of my LIFE
Quickie in an Elevator,
GOING DOWN?
Into the Garden
The Book Case
The Other Women
Menage a WHAT?

LARGE Print Novels

SHIPS CompanionSHIP, FriendSHIP,
RelationSHIP
Erotica Volume 1
Long Distance Romance
Children of Another Mother
Bikini's Are Dangerous
The Complete Series
Malice Masterpieces
The First Five Books
To Love a Shooting Star
The Claim
Represented
Timed Romance

K'ANNE MEINEL

Machiavellian

Malice

ISBN-13: 978-1959436065

K'Anne Meinel is available for comments at KAnneMeinel@aim.com as well as on Facebook, Google +, or her blog @ http://kannemeinel.wordpress.com/ or on Twitter @ kannemeinelaim.com, or on her website @ www.kannemeinel.com if you would like to follow her to find out about stories and book's releases.

www.shadoepublishing.com

ShadoePublishing@gmail.com

Shadoe Publishing is a United States of America company
Cover by: K'Anne Meinel
Edited by: Deb Amia

Machiavellian Malice

PUBLISHER'S NOTE

MACHIAVELLIAN MALICE

Book 29

Alice sat up suddenly. She'd been dreaming, and the nightmare that had nearly taken her away was of Emily standing in front of one of the buildings they had burned down. It took her a minute to realize she was home in their bed, and Kathy was asleep beside her.

Kathy. Jeez, the day hadn't gone well as the medical staff poked and prodded her, took x-rays and scans, and drew blood. They couldn't figure out why she was having so many problems, and her breathing was becoming more and more ragged as they argued about what course of treatment to give her. She hadn't been sleeping well, mostly because they had stayed out late in order to take the war to their enemy. Last night had been too close.

Alice lay down again as she thought over the warehouse fire. They'd taken out a drug factory, and she knew Artum would make someone pay for that. They had thrown hundreds of thousands of dollars in cash at the women, and she hoped they would use it wisely, but she also wondered how many of those six women were addicted to the drugs they had been packaging? How many of them would really escape the plight she was certain they hadn't asked to be thrown into? One or more of them would most likely go back into the only life they knew, and they would certainly point a finger towards the two women they had seen with the teen.

God, Emily had seen so much last night. There had been no answers from the shocked teen about what they should do with her. Alice had reluctantly driven them home, stopping at a big box store to dispose of some of the evidence in the SUV, stowing it in various garbage bins far from the scene of the crime and in places she knew there were no cameras. Kathy and Emily wanted to help her, but Kathy was coughing too much and would draw attention to them, and Alice was so angry about Emily, she waved her back into the SUV. She would normally have taken the rest of the evidence to the house in the valley but didn't want to take Emily there.

She thought about the threat that man Iggy had made against their daughter, her Emily, the daughter of her heart. She loved Kit too, but Emily was her blood. She knew without a doubt that this was her child from her and Kathy's unique mixing. She wouldn't have allowed her beloved daughter to be taken into prostitution and end up like those women, virtual slaves to…. And that was when Alice thought of the clinic that had saved Emily. She nearly sat up again to wake Kathy. They must take her to see Doctor Wilkerson.

* * * * *

"I don't understand why these people were in there, but this was definitely a front for a drug lab," the crime scene investigator stated, pointing back at the smoldering ruins of a once large warehouse. "Why was that one handcuffed to a desk?"

The Los Angeles Police Department, the Los Angeles Fire Department, the Drug Enforcement Administration (DEA), and a few other acronyms, including the FBI, were all very, very interested in this fire—even above all the other suspicious fires they had been investigating lately.

* * * * *

"You think Alice Weaver is involved in these suspicious fires in LA?" someone brought up as they discussed their current caseloads.

"Why not?" he shrugged. "She's not doing much online," he pointed to the computer that was monitoring the stocks Alice was buying on the internet, at least the ones they could find. Things had been rather quiet for a long time. What they didn't know was those were dummy stocks, and their own computer was giving them false information. Alice had no reason to invest anymore if she didn't want to. She had enough money to last the rest of her life, enough even to last the rest of her children's lives. If she wanted, her money would last several lifetimes for several generations. The amount of stocks she bought were small in comparison to what she already owned, which provided a legal income she could claim on her taxes. She'd bought a few things just for a write-off. She'd also bought a few stocks just to bring monies into the country that she could now claim.

* * * * *

Artum was convinced it was Alice Weaver setting the blazes that were costing him so much money. It was right after her ask and his refusal that these things started happening to his properties, so he started investigating her. Reading about the house she had purchased in Malibu, which was already on the market, didn't interest him. But the house in Palos Verdes fascinated him. He even found the original listing that read:

A private estate located in the prestigious Palos Verdes Estates offers resort style living at its best! This secluded estate boasts sensational panoramic views of the Pacific Ocean from almost every room of the home. A total renovation was designed and completed by the famous architect Don Hendrickson during the last three years. This renovation is a perfect balance of refinement and resort style living. This estate will exceed all your expectations, from the grand curb appeal and a huge lobby to a spacious living room and formal dining room. Also includes a great master suite, gourmet kitchen, fantastic library, multi-function media/ family room, two staff quarters with their own kitchen/ laundry/ dining facilities, N/S tennis court with ocean views, wine /cigar cellar, fantastic semi outdoor gym with its own bath and two separate garages with space for a total of 9 cars! The park-like grounds are lavishly designed and surrounded by 3 sides of parkland. This is one of a very few contemporary styled architectural estates on the hill, with big windows filled with sunlight and views! Please do not miss this grand estate, which has so much to offer!

He would have sent his guys to watch the house but didn't want them to get too interested in it yet. He knew the address as Alice had even given

it to them to rescue Kathy, which they had failed at with her refusal. He had to play it cool. He couldn't let anyone know that a woman was besting him. And then, he was informed that one of his holding companies had suffered another loss, one of their biggest to date. The lab had gone up in flames with Richard Pasternack and several of their guards inside. No mention was made of the women they had working in the lab. How in the hell had anyone found out that he owned that building? It hadn't been on Sebastian's rolls. He had owned it under another company name. Did Alice Weaver have people investigating him? He recalled things Sebastian had told him, how she had come into his homes, wherever he might be. Was she the cause of all these problems? He had higher-ups that he had to make payments to; he couldn't afford this embarrassment. The people he reported to would want answers…no, they would *demand* answers.

He couldn't fathom that this petite blonde was capable of the things he suspected. She had to have someone working for her. If he could prove she was behind these setbacks, he would destroy her and her family. If Alice could have read his thoughts, his life would already be in jeopardy.

* * * * *

"We've identified the body that was handcuffed in the office. The dental records indicate it's one Richard Pasternack. He lived in Palos Verdes Estates with his wife, a nurse that works in hospice care. She hasn't been working, but they also own…" the voice droned on in the meeting. Those listening were falling into a stupor until they heard, "her daughter was involved in a scandal at school. Remember those pictures that were circulating of Alice Weaver's daughter, Emily?" Several people perked up with that information, exchanging looks as notes were rapidly

made on that information as well as on the report the speaker was reviewing. It would be passed up the chain of command in the police department, the DEA, the FBI, and eventually, the CIA since Madelyn Korbel had flagged anything with Alice Weaver's name on it. Then, he casually mentioned, "They lived down the street from Alice Weaver's estate in Palos Verdes." That had many in the meeting scrambling to connect the dots.

* * * * *

Kathy agreed they should go see Doctor Wilkerson, but she was already feeling depressed about the many tests that Doctor Lenoir had ordered for her. However, Wilkerson had been able to cure Emily, and Alice had the utmost faith in him, so it couldn't hurt to go see him and get his opinion on the many tests ordered.

"Alice and Kathy, it is so good to see you," he said in greeting.

"Doctor Wilkerson," Alice returned, shaking his outstretched hand.

"Surely, you aren't here to talk about the dividend paperwork that just went out? The quarterly–" he began, but Alice cut him off.

"No, we are here for you to examine Kathy," she nodded towards her wife.

Kathy smiled and would have let Alice continue, but Alice stayed strangely quiet, letting her wife tell the doctor what she had been feeling: the fatigue, the cough, and what Doctor Lenoir had found.

"So, you thought they were speckles or like the measles?" he asked after a while as she described the x-rays she had seen.

"Yes, the dots were very prevalent," she noted, and Alice nodded in agreement.

"But you haven't been working with any chemicals, asbestos, or similar substances prior to this?" he asked astutely, taking notes as he listened.

Alice and Kathy both thought about the gasoline they had played with in the past week and shook their heads. Everyone knew that too much gas might be a carcinogen; however, this was too much and too soon. The spots inside Kathy's body were older than her exposure to that flammable material. Kathy briefly remembered Alice telling her that she could have put a match out in the gasoline, that it was the vapors that burned, not the fluid itself. It had seemed funny at the time.

"I'm going to need the other doctors to send over their tests results, so if you would sign here," Doctor Wilkerson produced an authorization paper, "...unless you want to go through those tests again?"

Both women shook their heads. Neither wanted Kathy to be subjected to a battery of duplicate tests.

"Do you think it's cancer?" Kathy asked him, sounding almost hopeless.

"I won't know until I see the results. I'll send this off immediately," he said, handing the signed form to a tech who worked for him. "Send that to L.A. Medical and then, follow up in half an hour with a phone call. I want those results immediately," he told the woman, who nodded as she hurried off. "I may have to run a few tests of my own," he warned Kathy, then patted her hand. "We'll find out what's going on and get you the appropriate treatment," he promised.

They both felt strangely relieved as they left the high-tech lab of Doctor Wilkerson. He had pulled off a miracle for Emily, but they both hoped that whatever was wrong with Kathy wasn't anything like that.

* * * * *

They started packing for Kit's graduation at Stanford. The four of them would be flying up to San Francisco and renting a car to drive in. Kit was so excited that she was graduating with honors, and Alice had teased her for not being valedictorian. The young woman explained because she had changed her major and gone to school one year too many, she wasn't eligible for that honor. The fact that she had been accepted to Harvard for her master's program was honor enough.

"I won't promise to be valedictorian there either," she teased Alice when she told her.

"Happy, healthy, and well-educated...I couldn't be prouder," Alice told her sincerely as she gave her a bear hug, remembering the young, frightened girl that had come to live with her so long ago. Her heart squeezed painfully seeing how much the girl looked like Kathy. She was reminded of her own sister's graduation from this same school so long ago. Kathy and Connie had been here together, along with Portia and Andie. Only immediate family were asked to the graduation ceremonies and even for family, four tickets was the max.

Kathy cried unashamedly as Kit's name was called and she walked across the stage to receive her diploma. Sean snapped pictures with the digital camera. They had been asked not to clap or whoop to prevent the ceremony from dragging on too long and to allow everyone's names to be heard. At the end though, after the last graduate had been called, the students had all thrown their caps into the air and whooped and hollered. The audience rose to cheer and stomp along with the graduates.

After the ceremony, Alice took the family to one of the best restaurants in San Francisco to celebrate. As they reminisced, she was so pleased to

see her family together and felt herself tearing up. Near the end of the night, Kit took her aside and asked about Kathy's cough.

"Oh, it's nothing. We took her to the doctor, and they haven't found anything," she told her daughter airily, having agreed with Kathy that they would tell this story to their children for now.

They all helped Kit load up her vehicle the next day. Alice realized everything wasn't going to fit, so she went to go get a U-Haul and trailer. They repacked what they could in the small truck and put the car on the trailer, so Kit could drive it back east. She had a small apartment there that Alice had bought for her, so she could intern that summer and then go to school at Harvard in the fall. She could have stayed in the dorms but felt it was too much to put up with the underclassmen and their antics at her age. Neither mother saw any signs of the boyfriend Kit had mentioned, and they decided not to ask. They would wait for her to tell them about him when she was ready. After everything was loaded, Kit went out for another meal with her family. She was sad to say goodbye to Stanford. It had been such a big part of her life for so long.

"Did you say goodbye to your friends, honey?" Kathy asked, putting her arm around Kit's shoulders as she gazed at the building the young woman had lived in these past years.

"Yeah, we had a party the other night to say our goodbyes. I didn't think some of them would even make it to graduation," she grinned, pleased she'd had the experience. She'd been one of the lucky ones. Alice had ensured there were no outstanding student loans for her to repay, and the generous allowance had made things easier for her than many of her fellow students. Now, she had a nice, solid car she was towing back east and a place to live when she got there. She knew she had it good.

"You know, if you need anything, you can just call," Alice said, looking at the woman who was now taller than Kathy but still looked just like her.

"Always, Momma A," she said as she let Kathy's hand fall from her shoulders to envelop the smaller woman in her arms. Alice had always been there for her; she barely remembered the time before Alice had entered her life. She deliberately erased the thoughts of when Alice had been missing for a time while she was in college.

Alice slipped her an envelope with cash and a debit card, and she whispered, "Call if you need more."

Kit grinned. Alice already paid her credit card off every month. She didn't need more, and she wasn't greedy.

Everyone waved as Kit set off. She wanted to get to at least Sacramento or even Reno before she stopped for the night. She had plenty of cash, a credit card, and a debit card as well, all thanks to her parents.

"You know, we never got to go on that vacation with the RV because of that internship Kit got," Sean commented.

"Ah, but that is where you are wrong...sorta," Alice told him with a smile, looking up at her strapping son with pride. He towered over all of them. The football practices gave his muscles ample opportunity to grow, and with his voracious appetite, he seemed to never stop growing. Alice was certain his long legs were hollow. He was a fine-looking specimen of manhood, growing out of the pimples that had plagued him and into a man she was proud of. He wasn't very attractive but had rugged looks and a steady look in his eye.

"I am? How?"

"Well, rather than camping, how about we drive from here and go see Mount Shasta and the area around it? Maybe we could go up to the

Redwoods too? No one has to be back for school," she added, since they were out for summer, "and your Mom and I would like to take you up there."

"Oh boy," Emily enthused. She'd been quiet for a while now, ever since the night she had snuck into her mother's SUV and been transported to the warehouse where they proceeded to burn it down, killing all who were in it. She realized Richard Pasternack had been a bad man, but she hadn't expected her mothers to kill him in that way. She'd heard that the Pasternacks had a funeral for him, but of course she couldn't go. She was conflicted about her feelings for Carmen. The girl had been so nasty to her. She hated her, and yet, at one time, she had been her best friend. This vacation sounded good. "I didn't pack enough," she informed her mothers.

"That's why I repacked your bag after you were done," Kathy laughed, coughed, and looked at Sean with a grin. She'd repacked his bags too.

* * * * *

Alice was sitting on the bench along the bluffs, looking out at the Pacific Ocean. She was waiting for Kathy to join her when she heard smaller footsteps and looked over to see Emily.

"Mom, I have questions," she stated unnecessarily.

Alice sighed. She'd been expecting this and knew that the teen had been very patient, waiting for punishments that never came. With the graduation and other events in their lives, she had wondered when Em would take the time to make sure they were alone and could talk. Kathy and she had both waited, wondering if the teen were shell shocked and would need therapy. "I'm sure you do," she said mildly.

Em grinned, then that turned into a grimace. "I really don't know how to say this…" she hesitated, clearly uncomfortable.

"I'm sure there is a lot you've been thinking about," Alice understated. She wouldn't start the ball rolling. The teen had to ask all by herself; she wasn't about to volunteer information.

"Mr. Pasternack…" she began. "I heard what he said. He was a bad man?" She felt foolish putting it like that, sounding like a child, but Alice intimidated her sometimes. She'd heard what he told Alice about where to find money. She hadn't understood it all, but it was enough, and with what happened later, she understood that he was laundering money for someone. She hadn't told Alice or Kathy that she'd heard him talking before she entered the office too, having listened unashamedly before making her presence known. She couldn't understand it. When she had hung out with Carmen, her father and mother had been so kind, charming even.

Alice nodded. She could hear the little girl in her teenager. Just in the time since Alice had come home, Em had grown as she healed from the blood disease. She had caught herself eyeing her daughter, speculating about her time and again, wondering at the woman she was about to become.

"Did he have to die? Did he deserve to die?"

"I sometimes think some people are born to die," Alice said cryptically, parroting something she had heard in an old western. At the teen's startled look, she clarified, "Some people choose to be evil…some are born that way."

"Do you think Mr. Pasternack was born bad or chose it?"

"I think he got caught up with all the money made by the drugs. That business wasn't about the wholesale goods they imported, it was about the

drugs they brought in and distributed. I didn't even know about the drugs until he told us."

Em thought for a while and then asked, "Did he launder the money for them?"

Alice was surprised by how astute and how calm the teen was. They were in this picturesque part of California, and the park was absolutely beautiful. They were parked near a cabin she had rented; within a half hour of the mighty redwoods they would be seeing again tomorrow. Now, they were just relaxing. At least she had been relaxing until her daughter decided she needed answers. "Yes," she nodded, "he laundered money and more. He obviously knew what he was doing. He invested funds for them. He knew where the money was coming from and where it went."

"There was a lot of cash in that bag," the teen mused. "Why didn't you keep it?"

"Because those women needed it and deserved it," Alice replied, wondering what else the teen would ask. She certainly hadn't wanted any of those funds. She also didn't need them but wouldn't tell the teen that.

"Do you think they will share it or…get caught or…" the teen wasn't sure what she was asking, and she was obviously being influenced by the TV shows she had watched over the years.

Alice smiled, showing off even, white teeth that had all been replaced over the years. "Some might be smart enough to get out of there. Some might get caught, and they will mention the women who freed them. You can never talk about this…" she began, wondering if this was too much to burden her daughter with. The child already had several secrets she had been told to keep for her parents.

"I know how to keep a secret, Mom," the beleaguered teen said in a tone that had Alice smiling again.

"I know you do, honey, but it's a habit of mine to remind you."

"How do you know the women weren't there voluntarily?" Emily asked, surprising Alice with the question.

"I suspect they were taken prisoner in Russia and transported here, then their passports were confiscated, or something like that. If they weren't useful in prostitution, they had to be useful in other ways."

"Even with masks on, I bet they inhaled that stuff," Em stated astutely, remembering the scene in that horrible room where the women were working in all the dust. Even she knew what it was.

Alice nodded sagely. "I hope you never have to see that stuff again," she stated, a warning buried within the statement.

"Don't worry, Mom. I don't like drugs," she assured her.

"Oh really?" Alice asked, wondering at the meaning in the teen's statement.

"Well, after what Carmen and her friends pulled last year, I don't want anything to do with drugs or alcohol."

Alice nodded. That made sense.

"I mean, maybe when I'm older and I know what I'm doing, I might like a drink or something," she continued, "but nothing in excess like that ever again." She shuddered at the memory of seeing her vulnerable self in those photos and hearing what people had said about her. So many lies. She hated Carmen for that!

"Well, when you are an adult, you will have a lot of decisions to make for yourself. I just hope you are responsible about them," Alice advised. She too remembered the photos of her daughter and the rage she had felt against the teen who had taken them. She had worked so hard to erase those photos, although they seemed unending as people stored them on their private computers and shared them occasionally. The only thing that

had helped her feel better were the pictures she had posted that contained viruses and would destroy people's hard drives if they were stupid enough to download the whole picture. This conversation wasn't going at all as she had thought it would.

"What if I was one of those women?" the teen asked suddenly, after a long period of quiet reflection while gazing out at the beautiful view before the sun set.

"Which women?" Alice asked, confused and glancing around hoping to see who Emily was referring to.

"Those women in the drug factory…" the teen began.

Alice suddenly understood, and her face changed. She wasn't about to tell Em what the men had said about her. It could so easily have *been* her. "I'd have been very sad for you. It can't be an easy life when they are addicted to that stuff. And if they get too old for the work, are they done away with?"

"I bet those men who use them don't care. They are just after the money."

Alice nodded. This teen was right on the mark, but she wasn't about to ask how she knew. She obviously had thought this out.

"Did Mr. Pasternack deserve to die?" the teen wondered aloud again.

"I think he did," Alice said softly and watched the teen nod. "Are you feeling bad for him, honey?"

"I think I feel bad for Carmen. Despite what she did, he was her father, and he loved her."

Alice understood. Carmen had been Em's best friend for a while. It had been a setup from the get-go, but the teen hadn't realized it until it was too late.

Em leaned into Alice. It was a bit cool here on the bench looking out over the water. The fog was rolling in, and neither of them had a jacket or a sweater. "Do you know how many people you have killed?" Em asked in a subdued voice.

Alice froze momentarily but not so long that the teen would notice. She had been thinking how nice it was that her daughter still wanted to cuddle and had put her arm around her. She remembered the little girl who had put her head into Alice's neck with her arm slung across her chest and around the other side of her neck. It had been an endearing habit of the little girl. Alice had relished those moments alone with her daughter. Now, Emily was on the cusp of womanhood and demanding answers that Alice wasn't so sure she wanted to or should answer. "No, I didn't keep count," she admitted honestly.

Emily thought about that, wondering how many people her mother had killed. She'd heard about Kazakhstan from her mother's own lips. Now, having seen what she did to Mr. Pasternack, she wondered that she wasn't shocked about it.

"I don't just kill willy-nilly," Alice downplayed, looking at her semi-horrified, semi-fascinated daughter. "I need to justify any killings in my mind. I need to know there is a purpose…a reason."

Emily nodded. She too had felt that Mr. Pasternack deserved to die, but she wondered why she felt bad for Carmen, who had hurt her so badly. "Are you a psychopath?"

"No."

"How do you know?"

"A psychopath lacks empathy. I don't kill randomly; I only kill if it's necessary."

Had it been necessary to kill Mr. Pasternack and that guard? Thinking about the gun the man had held on them reminded her of the men who had broken into their home and touched her. She shuddered slightly and Alice felt it.

"Cold?" she asked, wondering if they should head in. She wanted Emily to stop asking questions, and at the same time, she wanted to answer whatever questions the teen might have. She instinctively knew this wasn't the end of her questions.

"Yeah, but I don't want to go in yet. I never knew Mom was your accomplice," Emily told her.

"Accomplice?" Alice asked, feeling a challenge to the word.

"All this time, I thought she was just your housewife. You know," she added, seeing Alice's expression, "keeping the house straight, raising your kids, washing the laundry?"

Alice chuckled. That was why they had a housekeeper. Kathy did whatever the heck she wanted, had unlimited funds, and loved her. This child of their love couldn't understand, not this young. "Your mother," she began carefully, unsure if it was fair to speak for Kathy, "is not a murderess. A true murderer deludes themselves that the killings were justified or deserved. There is only one reason to kill: to protect yourself and save innocent lives."

"Is that why you killed?" she asked.

Alice nodded, and added so the teen would hear her, "Yes. I believe I have saved people with my actions." She didn't add that some killings were for revenge and to prevent the people from doing again whatever it was that had pissed her off.

"Then, by your own definition, you are a murderer," the teen stated. Alice's facial expression changed slightly. "You have deluded yourself that the killing was justified or deserved," she quoted.

Alice chuckled. She'd have to be on her toes with this child of hers. The teen was very quick, and she had both her mothers' brains.

"Are you going to kill Mrs. Pasternack?" the teen asked.

"Do I have a reason to?" she asked in return, hedging. She was beginning to suspect a lot about Sandi Pasternack. Alice was certain she was a killer acting under the guise of a healthcare worker who helped in hospice. The look in the woman's eyes was enough; Alice recognized another killer. She'd seen her own eyes and read what they told her.

The teen shrugged. "I just wondered if she, you know…was on your hit list?"

Alice laughed and shook her head. "I don't have a hit list."

"Oh," the teen sat back, cuddling into the warmth that Alice's body generated. She sounded almost disappointed.

"Have you ever killed a child?" she asked and felt the tension in her mother's body, even though she tried to hide it.

"Not that I know of," Alice answered honestly and then turned the questions on her daughter. "Do you want me to kill Carmen?"

"Would you?" Em sounded both horrified and fascinated at the idea.

Without hesitation Alice answered, "No." Nothing more, no explanation, just a simple, 'No."

"Why not?"

"Because I am holding onto the belief that there is hope for that girl," she lied. Based on her observations, that kid was seriously screwed up and would only continue to hurt others. "I don't kill children," she finished quietly.

"But after what she did…" the teen began defensively.

"She deserves to be punished, but not a final punishment, and not by me."

"What if she came at me to kill me?"

"Then, I would defend you to the best of my ability," Alice told her and hoped that was the end of the conversation. It was making her distinctly uncomfortable.

Emily waited a while and then asked, "Do you think you and Mom will ever break up again?"

Alice could sense a lot of meaning in that one question. She knew the last few years had made them all a little uneasy. "Your Mom and I have come a long way. We've worked hard to make this lifelong commitment. It's not what everyone thinks it is. It's not waking up early every day and making breakfast, so we can eat together. It's not even cuddling in bed until we fall asleep together. It isn't the clean home, which I might add Mrs. Fernandez contributes to," she teased, and the teen grinned. Kathy had taught them all to clean up after themselves, so Mrs. Fernandez didn't have to do everything. "It's about someone who steals the covers and snores like a chainsaw. Sometimes it's about the slammed doors, words we didn't mean to say, and even the silent treatment we give each other as our hearts are trying to heal. The most important thing to learn from all that is to forgive. If you don't come back to forgiveness, then there really wasn't a relationship in the first place." She let the teen digest all that before she continued, "I love coming home to the same person. Your mother knows that I love and care about her and about all of you. All our anger and all our foibles make us who we are. It's about laughing together over something hilariously funny or even something we did that was stupid. It isn't about finger pointing or assigning blame but about helping

each other become the best we can be. That goes for your mother, for you, your brother, and your sister. All of you. I didn't leave because I wanted to leave. I left because your Mom needed that time apart. I hadn't planned on leaving for quite that long though," she finished wryly, and Emily chuckled.

"I don't know that I'll ever have what you and Mom have," she stated sadly, and Alice immediately felt a sense of foreboding.

"Why do you say that?" She wanted to tell her daughter she was too young to feel that way but didn't want to dismiss or belittle her feelings at such a tender age.

"I can't imagine trusting anyone that much."

Alice felt bad about that. Carmen had betrayed her on so many levels. She wondered if Emily had had a crush on the little twit and that was part of the hurt. "Living with the person you love is amazing. It's an experience I hope you have someday, and you will find it was worth the wait. It might not come when you want it, but if it does come, I hope you are open to it. I didn't think I'd find it either," she confessed, and the teen looked at her, startled. "I was alone a long time, dating but not looking for a long-term relationship...and then, your mom came along."

"Why did you marry Mom? She's nothing like you."

Alice smiled, remembering the night she had proposed to Kathy. "Have I ever told you about the night I proposed to your mom?" she asked the teen.

Emily shook her head.

"Maybe this should wait? It's getting cold out here," Alice offered, but the teen shook her head vehemently, snuggling in closer to Alice's warmth.

"No, I want to hear. Please tell me," the teen pleaded, wanting a confirmation of the love between her two mothers.

"Okay, but I'm only going over the highlights," Alice told her and began to tell her story. "Remember the gazebo in our backyard?" At the teen's nod. she continued. Kathy had gasped as they arrived at the gazebo. Dozens of flowers—roses, lilies, and many she couldn't even name—were in pots, planters, and vases all over the gazebo. A bottle of champagne stood in a large champagne bucket with two glasses sticking up out of the ice. "What's this?" she asked in wonderment as she turned to look in the amused eyes of Alice.

"This is a celebration," Alice responded, adding *I hope* in her head. She let go of Kathy's hand to reach for the champagne and step into the gazebo. To her satisfaction, Kathy followed her, as she had hoped she would.

"A celebration of what?" Kathy looked around, amazed at all the flowers and admiring their beautiful bouquets. The odor alone was almost overwhelming, but the sheer mass of blooms took her breath away.

Letting go of the champagne, Alice turned and grasped both of Kathy's hands. She got down on one knee and saw the apprehension begin in Kathy's face.

"Kathy, I'd like to make this official. Will you marry me?"

Kathy just stared at her for the longest time.

For the first time in a long time, Alice felt nervous. Fear was almost clutching at her heart. The longer Kathy took to answer Alice's question, the more Alice felt like she was strangling. She tried to wait patiently, but the silence was beginning to kill her. She realized she had never felt this way before, at least not from this side of the situation.

Kathy finally blinked after what seemed like ages. She realized Alice had set the stage for this proposal and how truly romantic it was. She swallowed as tears welled in her eyes at the incredibly romantic gesture. She was having trouble speaking as she started to nod, blubber, and say, "Yyyyes, I'll marry you, Alice," and yanked Alice into her arms, burying her head in Alice's neck as she sobbed.

For once in her life, a woman's tears didn't confuse her. She understood the emotions Kathy was experiencing right now. If she could have, she would have cried with her, but life had long ago killed the thing inside her that allowed tears to fall. She could only hold Kathy tightly and hope she understood she felt the same emotions as she rocked her.

Slowly, and after a long time, Kathy's tears of joy stopped, and she pulled back, her face a mess. "This is so beautiful," she hiccupped.

Alice smiled as she reached in her pocket for the ring she had searched for that morning. "Then, will you accept this as a token of my love for you?" she asked formally, remembering some movie that had used those same exact words.

Kathy gaped at the beautiful diamond she saw in her love's hand. It was flawless, as far as she could see, and the ring her husband had given her was half the size of this incredible stone. She held out her left hand, and Alice slipped it on her ring finger. It fit perfectly, and she stared at it a long moment before taking Alice in her arms once again and hugging her tight. "Thank you. I love you sooo much!" she sobbed once again.

It was a long time before they sampled the champagne and made toasts to each other and a long life together. They talked over plans of having a small ceremony. It had become legal once again in the state of California for same-sex couples to marry, so their plans wouldn't have to wait. They made several trips to carry the containers of flowers into the house, placing

them all over the house and filling it with the delightful aroma of roses, lilies, and other varieties of flowers that Alice's romantic proposal had wrought. But before they brought everything into the house, Kathy had insisted on taking pictures of the gazebo filled with the flowering bonanza. She had then called Mrs. Fernandez to take a picture of the two women amongst the flowering blooms. The three of them carried armloads of blooms into the house and placed them on every available flat surface.

"This is going to make the house smell like a flower shop," Mrs. Fernandez teased as Kathy showed her the ring. She was pleased for the couple. She didn't understand their relationship, but she liked weddings. She and Kathy excitedly made plans.

Alice watched and laughed at their excitement. She hoped Kit would like the idea too.

"Kit told me she was just so glad you two would be together forever, but she never shared all the details of your engagement," Emily said to her mom, delighting in the story. She had seen the pictures of course, and she had always wondered at them. "She loves calling you Mama Al," she teased, knowing it was funny.

Alice smiled.

"I didn't remember it all quite like that," Kathy suddenly spoke up behind them. She'd come up very quietly on the path, intending to tell them to come in as it was getting cold with the fog rolling in. Hearing Alice tell the teen about the night she had proposed had halted her progression, and she was pleased to hear her wife tell it so well.

Alice turned, wondering how long her wife had been there. She was looking a little bit frail to Alice's knowing eyes. She smiled, not letting on in the least how concerned she was for Kathy's health.

Kathy looked at Alice. Those amazing eyes captivated as much today as they had so long ago. They looked at her and made her feel beautiful, and that was all that mattered.

"Mom, you two are lucky to have found each other," Emily said succinctly.

Kathy nodded and looked at her daughter as she got up from the bench. "We are indeed. Yes, we are indeed," she answered as Alice came and slipped her hand around Kathy's waist to walk her back to the cabin. Being shorter, she couldn't quite rest her head on Kathy's shoulder comfortably, but she could breathe quietly into her ear as she whispered, "I love you."

Kathy squeezed where she was holding onto Alice as she walked with her daughter and wife.

* * * * *

"Spouses can't testify against spouses," he pointed out.

"Does that apply to same-sex spouses?" someone asked.

"What do you mean?" Madelyn interjected, looking up from the paperwork they had been previewing and fixing the speaker with an intense look.

"Well," he looked uncomfortable to be asked such a straight-forward question in the group meeting, "it's not like it's a *real* marriage, you know, between a guy and some chick."

There were quite a few muffled laughs, and Marilyn looked at the man like he was insane. "So, you are saying two women or two men married to each other could testify against their companion because a marriage between same-sex partners isn't real?"

"Yeah, something like that," he answered, and he sounded earnest.

"You," she said, pointing at the man, "go…leave. You're off this task force!" She pointed at the door.

"*What?* What did I say?" he asked, spreading his hands in confusion.

Madelyn rose so she was towering over the table. Leaning forward on her hands to make her point, she replied, "If you have to ask that question, you're too stupid to be on this task force." She gestured to the paperwork everyone had brought to the meeting, "We don't want you here if you are so narrow-minded you might miss things. So, I'm asking you *nicely*," she said in a menacing voice, "to leave." She gestured at the door once more.

He looked around at the other agents, mostly the men. Several avoided his look, but a couple stared at him with incredulous looks. Gathering his notes, he stood up.

"No, you won't be needing those," Director Wolf told him quietly from his seat in the corner where he had been observing. Gesturing at the paperwork, he said, "Leave that."

Embarrassed now, he made his way around the long table and exited through the door, being careful to close it gently behind himself.

There was silence in the room for a full thirty seconds before Wolf looked over at Madelyn and asked, "Doesn't that only matter if it wasn't in furtherance of a crime?"

Since there wasn't any proof that Alice Weaver had actually committed any crime, that was a moot point. Madelyn's eyes narrowed as she contemplated what Wolf might know that she didn't know before answering, "Well, unless we can prove a crime was committed, there is no way we could apply any pressure on Kathy Weaver, even if she *would* testify against Alice. Furthermore, due to the length of time they've been married, I doubt she'd give her up." She didn't add that Kathy probably

knew what side her bread was buttered on, but she had met the mouse, saw the way she looked at Alice adoringly, and knew in her gut they would never be able to convince the woman to testify. Kathy would plead the fifth, and she had enough money to hire an army of the best lawyers to keep her out of trouble. Thinking about it, Madelyn knew there was no way Kathy could have been involved in any of Alice's wrongdoings.

* * * * *

"So, it's cancer then?" Kathy asked despondently as Doctor Wilkerson finished telling them what he had found after he did a few more tests on her.

He nodded after glancing at Alice as though asking for her permission. He licked his lips before continuing, "Yes, and it's an aggressive form of cancer that does not have any of the more obvious marker signs to show what kind of cancer it is or what kinds it is developing into."

"Kinds?" Alice asked, narrowing her eyes at the word.

He nodded again, gulping at the unwelcome news he would have to impart, but he knew better than to keep anything from their generous benefactor. Alice had invested in them when no one else would. For the sake of their company, he couldn't afford to piss off her or her wife. "Yes, it's mutating rapidly, and we can't tell you what kind it will become next, but it's already in her lungs, breast, and the lymph nodes."

"Upper or lower?" Alice asked, seemingly ignoring the indrawn breath of her wife, who had gasped at the idea of breast cancer.

"Both," he answered, realizing she might know more about cancer than he thought. "I can pinpoint where it entered the body, but I can't figure out where it's going since it's mutating so rapidly. Just in the week since

Dr. Lenoir took these," he indicated the tests that had been sent over, "and mine here," he indicated the other folder, "it's spread and grown."

"Wait! You can tell *how* it entered my body?" Kathy asked, surprised.

He nodded.

"How?" Alice asked, almost angrily. She was holding Kathy's hand, as though to keep from striking the man as they waited for the information to come from his mouth.

"There is a striking array of cells that are focused around her hand and move up her arm to her lungs. From there, I believe it went to her breasts and lymph nodes…" he began, pointing at the upper body x-rays to show the small white dots, but Alice and Kathy had exchanged a look, and then, Kathy looked down at her hand, the one clasped in Alice's.

"What can we do about it?" Alice asked practically, controlling herself…but just barely.

"We will start an aggressive form of chemo to halt the growth but I–"

"What if I do nothing?" Kathy asked suddenly, shocking them all.

Recovering first, Doctor Wilkerson said sadly, "Then you will most certainly die."

Alice turned to Kathy inquiringly, but she wouldn't look at her. Kathy was focused on the doctor. "How long?"

He swallowed. "I'd say about four months, maybe five, but I have to advise you to fight. It will be a horrible death otherwise, and I believe you will smother," he gestured to her breasts and the lungs beneath them.

"Kathy, you've got to fight," Alice almost pleaded with her, looking at her intensely.

Kathy looked in Alice's amazing eyes and was surprised to see tears welling up. This made her want to cry as well. She nodded almost

absentmindedly. She would fight. Oh yes, for this woman she would fight.

The ride home was particularly tense. Alice pulled over at a cliff overlooking the Pacific Ocean and looked out at the view before turning to her wife and pulling her into her arms. She sniffed her hair, luxuriating in the familiar smells of Kathy's body wash, shampoo, and conditioners. A hint of her perfume was so welcome now.

"I don't want to die," Kathy said in a frightened voice. "I want to live," she said as she pulled back to look at Alice. Her eyes were awash in tears, and Alice's tears were welling up but unshed.

"Then we fight!" Alice responded.

"Do you remember that pin prick I got in the lawyer's office from Sandi Pasternack's ring?" Kathy asked casually, watching Alice's reaction to head off what she thought might be a potential problem.

Alice remembered that incident in a flash. She too had been about to shake the woman's hand, but with Kathy exclaiming in pain, she'd refused. She remembered the look in Sandi's eyes…had that been disappointment? "You think that's when–?" she asked, but she agreed as Kathy nodded.

"It is concentrated in this hand," she indicated her right hand and looked at it as though it should be cut off. "But without proof…" she continued, looking up at her wife and seeing her eyes narrow in contemplation. She knew she was starting something she might not live to see. "We don't have proof," she almost pleaded.

"Then I will get the proof," Alice promised her. Her mind was already working on a plan to get into the Pasternack's home down the road from their own.

Angrily, Alice drove them home, cutting off an idiot who was driving too slowly. The next light halted her, giving the man she had cut off time to pull up next to them. He looked at them angrily and Kathy, on the same side he was on, shrugged and held her palms up in a helpless gesture. He indicated she should roll down her window. Stupidly, she complied.

"What the fuck is wrong with you, lady?" he shouted past her to Alice, ready to get out of his own car.

"Look, mister, my wife suffers from PTSD. She didn't mean anything by it," Kathy tried to explain.

Alice had turned when Kathy opened her window since the excellent air conditioning in the Rover gave her no need to open her window. She wondered if Kathy had passed gas or something, and then she saw the guy in the car next to theirs. She was ready to get out of her SUV in answer to his tone. Kathy reached over and put her hand on Alice's leg, squeezing warningly.

"Then she shouldn't be driving!" he shouted across the roar of the engines. Alice had put hers in park and was revving her engine, ready to put it in drive and speed away from this moron. At the feel of Kathy's hand on her leg, she put it into drive.

"I agree, but then, what am I going to do. Please forgive her," Kathy said sweetly and saw him calm down slightly.

Just then, the lights changed, and Alice roared off angrily, leaving the man coughing in her exhaust. She outdistanced him easily with the powerful engine of the Rover.

"Why'd you appease that moron?" Alice asked.

"Why'd you antagonize that moron?" Kathy countered saucily.

Alice started to laugh at the incongruity of their conversation. They'd had a bad, tension-filled day. She'd made it worse, and Kathy had told the

man she suffered from PTSD in order to defuse the situation. That was probably true with everything she had been through, but it was also funny. Kathy joined in, enjoying laughing with her wife.

* * * * *

Kathy started chemo, and the first dose, administered through an IV in her arm, seemed easy. It felt cold as it entered her vein. Doctor Wilkerson had offered to put a shunt in her chest to make it easier to administer the drugs. In fact, he had encouraged her to do so, but Kathy had refused.

"No, I won't have one of those things stuck in me," she indicated her chest where they wanted to implant the shunt. "You can use my veins; they're healthy," she said, holding out her arms to show the veins at the V in her arm.

"I don't think you understand what this will do to them–" he tried to explain, but Kathy cut him off.

"I know," she countered sadly. "They will scar and shrink, and you'll have to use other veins sometimes," she said resignedly, gesturing to her other arm. "I don't want a shunt."

He sighed quietly, not willing to argue. This treatment, while experimental, should help slow the growth and might even stop it. He'd called around to see who was in the latter parts of their studies doing clinical trials on humans and made sure Kathy Weaver did not get the placebo. He shuddered to think if they failed because Alice was one of their most vested benefactors.

"That's cold," Kathy complained as the liquid entered her arm. It looked odd, with a pale pink tint to it. They put warming blankets on

Kathy as Alice sat quietly by waiting for her, willing to fetch her anything as they watched the first bag of poisons drain into her body.

"Now, you are going to start feeling nauseous, and I want you to take…" Wilkerson droned on, prescribing various drugs that Kathy would have to take to counter the effects of the drugs they were pumping into her body to kill the cancer cells.

Alice went to the drive-thru at the pharmacy to fill all the prescriptions, and they waited. "How are you doing, babe?" she worried, looking over at Kathy, who was taking slow, cleansing breaths.

"I'm good. I think the nausea is starting, but maybe I should get something to eat?"

"Did you eat today?"

"Yes, I started with a banana and then, half an hour later, I had cereal, so I wouldn't have an empty stomach for this," she lifted her arm to show the spot where they had inserted the needle. It was covered by a small patch of cotton, and Kathy had been holding it in place rather than having tape applied. She claimed the tape ripped her skin, and she'd rather hold it herself. She gently removed it now with her fingertips, and it had stopped bleeding. It already looked like it was going to bruise.

"Then, we'll stop for lunch," Alice promised, looking back as the pharmacist's voice came over the tinny-sounding speaker.

"These prescriptions are for you?" he asked, looking at Alice with her punk rock hairdo, the blonde hair sticking up.

"No, they are for my wife," she said, indicating Kathy, who leaned forward so they could see each other. She raised her hand as though she were a schoolgirl in class.

"I'm going to need some identification. Some of these are pretty strong," he said disapprovingly.

Kathy mumbled under her breath about jackasses as she fumbled in her purse for her wallet and held up her driver's license.

"Please put it in the drop box and send it through," he intoned, squinting at her.

Alice took it and dropped it in, shoving hard on the receptacle so it went through with a bang. She saw him back away slightly as it shot through. She looked back innocently when he looked up, then he picked up the license and examined it carefully. He looked from the picture to Kathy, who was still leaning forward, comparing her with the photo. He looked suspicious as he examined both, then put the license back in the drawer and added some papers he had printed off and a pen.

"You need to sign for these," he told them as Alice gathered the things together. She handed everything to Kathy in case he was going to be a stickler about that.

Kathy sighed as she retrieved her license and began looking through the paperwork, all of it mostly for insurance purposes to prove they were receiving the drugs.

"That will be sixteen hundred and eighty dollars," he said as he bagged everything up after she returned the paperwork.

"Doesn't our insurance pay for all that?" Alice asked, hearing Kathy gasp in the background at the amount. The blonde was getting annoyed.

"Yes, they will reimburse you for this–" he began, but Alice interrupted.

"The normal procedure is to give the patient the meds they need and bill the insurance company," she clarified.

"Yes, but some of these may not be covered by–" he began, but she interrupted again.

"Then, you tell me which ones aren't covered, and we will get the insurance company and the doctor to iron that out. Meanwhile, my wife needs these meds to survive." She pointed at the bags of medicines they had watched him fill. "She has just started chemotherapy, and I don't think the doctor would be happy if she didn't comply by taking all the medicine he has prescribed." Alice looked behind her vehicle and saw a line of cars was forming behind her SUV. She could see the man behind them was becoming impatient.

"Ma'am, I don't set the–" he began again, but Alice was becoming impatient too.

"I'm not here to tell you how to make your policies or how to go about billing, but I'll wait while we straighten this out, so my wife can get the medicine her doctor clearly wants her to have," she said in a deceivingly polite voice.

He couldn't bluff her, and he too could see the line of cars forming behind her SUV. He turned off the microphone and looked towards someone else, discussing it with them. The person shrugged. He made a quick phone call while Alice watched him, a smile plastered on her face.

"Do you think he–?" Kathy began, but Alice shushed her under her breath.

"He's probably listening to us through that," she said in an aside, nodding slightly towards the microphone.

After what seemed an interminably long time—the guy behind them had started tapping on his horn, earning a glare from Alice—the pharmacist began putting the bags into the drawer, and he clicked on the microphone again. "We will bill your insurance company, but you are legally liable for any of these they don't pay for," he told them again in a disapproving voice.

"Thank you," Alice replied in a sugary, saccharine voice as she gathered the many bags, handing them to Kathy. As soon as she could, she drove away, tapping on the brakes to alarm the idiot behind her, who had rushed to fill her spot even before she drove off.

"Jeeze, how am I going to remember what to take and when," Kathy put in, looking at the many bags of medicines that Doctor Wilkerson had prescribed.

"We'll set up a medicine chart, maybe get one of those plastic pillbox things for daily doses or whatever. I think we might want to change our pharmacy though," Alice put in as she maneuvered around some traffic.

"You noticed the attitude too?"

"Oh yeahhh," she answered with a grin.

"I feel like having Carl's Jr.," Kathy mentioned.

"Grease?" Alice asked, concerned.

"Just the hamburger, no fries. A Dr. Pepper sounds good and maybe a salad?"

Alice would give her anything she wanted. She knew Kathy had to be feeling ill after all that poison was pumped into her veins, but she was hiding it remarkably well. Going through the drive-thru at Carl's was a lot less stressful than the one at the pharmacy. They parked in the parking lot to eat their lunch.

Kathy dug into her Western Bacon Cheeseburger sans cheese with gusto. "Mmm," she said as she took a sip of her ice-cold soda.

"You may regret that later," Alice said as she laughed at her wife's expression.

"I don't care," she returned, watching as Alice bit into her own hamburger and licked at the western sauce around her mouth enticingly. How could she feel like crap and be aroused by her wife at the same time?

Kathy enjoyed her meal, and she did regret it later. As soon as they were home, she snuck the many bags of medicine up to their bedroom and went right into the bathroom to throw up in the toilet. Everything she had just eaten came back up, along with anything she hadn't yet digested from breakfast. It took a long time before she finally had the dry heaves and then, she rinsed her mouth out with water. Immediately, she had to turn quickly and pull her pants down to sit on the throne and evacuate her bowels. It was horrible!

Alice stood by helplessly as her wife was sick in the bathroom. There was nothing she could do about it, so instead, she turned on a fan in the bedroom and opened a window, hoping her wife would appreciate the gesture and not be insulted. She headed down to the kitchen for some crackers and white soda. "Make sure you have lots of this on hand," she instructed their housekeeper as she hefted the packet of salted crackers and the soda she'd poured into a glass with ice.

Mrs. Fernandez nodded and said, "Yes, Ms. Alice." She wondered what was going on but didn't ask; it wasn't her place. A lot of odd things had happened in this house over the years that she pretended not to see or hear. It was a good job that paid well and even offered health insurance. She would do this job for as long as she was able.

Kathy had turned on the water in the shower and was washing her sweaty body and rinsing the acid from her backside. Despite the hot water, she was shivering and feeling miserable. It took a while before she turned off the water and wrapped herself in a fluffy white towel.

"Need help?" Alice asked from where she was standing by the door, feeling helpless.

"I need my robe," Kathy answered, her teeth chattering despite the heat and clouds of steam in the bathroom.

Alice handed her the fluffy robe she rarely used. Alice preferred the satin one but knew Kathy needed more than the thinness of that right now. She wasn't trying to be sexy; she just wanted to get warm. Alice helped rub her hair dry and tuck her into bed with her sweats on.

"Jeeze, how bad is this going to get?" Kathy mumbled as she carefully ate a cracker and sipped at the soda. "Thank you for this," she murmured, gesturing with the glass.

"Don't ask," Alice mumbled back with a smile, watching her. She'd done some research and knew it might get really bad really fast.

"Wonder if I'm going to lose my hair?" Kathy mused miserably as she looked at the long tendrils hanging over her shoulder.

"Think of the wonderful hats you can wear. You can even get a wig if you want." Alice tried to smile, making it sound like fun.

"Well, there is that," Kathy answered, burping ungracefully from the soda.

"Feeling any better?" Alice laughed at her wife who was usually much more polite and discreet about belching.

"Yeah, and I'm finally getting warm." She pulled a leg out from under the covers to cool down a little. "We're going to have to tell the kids," she stated, looking at Alice.

"How much of it do you want to tell them?"

Lowering her voice, Kathy asked, "How much have you found out?"

Lowering her own voice, Alice answered, "That twit is still pulling stunts, but her computer isn't hooked up to her mother's, and the mother's computer is not on a network. I'm going to have to figure out some other way to get the information I need."

Kathy knew the twit Alice was referring to was Carmen. They were both of the same opinion on that girl. She was bad news and heading for

worse. What she had pulled on their daughter was enough to set any parent off, and while they'd sued the Pasternacks and reached a settlement, this disease Kathy was fighting was not pleasant and certainly wasn't worth the money they had won and put in trust for their daughter. Furthermore, if Sandi's ring was the cause of this cancer, she had a lot to answer for.

* * * * *

"Are you dying?" Emily asked, her voice sounding like a little girl, not the teenager she had become. Sean looked on worriedly where his two moms were sitting on the couch explaining what was going on.

"I'm not gonna lie to you, Em. This is a going to be a rough road, and I could die," Kathy told her, wanting to take her in her arms but also knowing it had to be on the teen's terms. She could tell Sean was trying manfully not to cry, holding it in but looking devasted.

"But you're not old. You can't die," the teen continued.

Alice exchanged a look with Kathy. They had to remember this teenager was still young in many ways.

"I assure you, I can. I have before," she tried to joke but regretted it when the teen blanched. She'd been very young when Kathy had been taken before. Alice had just returned last year after being away, and they'd also thought she was dead. "But this time…" she continued, trying to forget the look on her daughter's face, "I'm going to fight." Alice took her hand to remind her wife she was there. "We," she amended, "are going to fight…together."

"Why didn't you tell us when you found out?" Sean asked. His voice was suspiciously odd.

"This all happened rather suddenly," Kathy told him. "Doctor Wilkerson had to find an experimental treatment to help me."

"He's good at that," Emily said resentfully.

Both of her parents looked at her. "Yes, he is. Thank goodness he is," Kathy agreed, remembering her fears for this youngest daughter of theirs. First, she had worried if she would be able to have her, and then later, she had worried if she would lose her to a mysterious blood disease. She looked at Alice, who squeezed her hand reassuredly. It was Alice's blood transfusion that had saved their daughter. "The cancer has spread fast, but he found a study that he believes may help me."

"What happens if it doesn't work?" Sean asked.

Alice studied her only son. He was trying to think things through logically and asking all the right questions. He was so close to being an adult. "Then we try something else," Alice answered quietly, drawing their kids' attention to her.

"Isn't there something we can do? Donate blood? Platelets?"

Alice shook her head. She wished it were that easy.

Kathy smiled. "We're going to follow Doctor Wilkerson's orders for now. I just wanted you two to know, since there is a good chance I will lose my hair and my appearance will be altered."

It was this revelation that had Emily getting up from her seat to take Kathy in her arms. "Oh, Mommy," she sobbed.

Alice exchanged a look with Sean and would have gone to him, but he fisted his hands and rubbed at his eyes as he rocked slightly. Her heart melted at his anguish. Their children had been through so much in their young lives. She looked at Kathy who was comforting their daughter, and Kathy released her hand and nodded towards Sean. Alice got up to put her arms around the young man, and he rose, brushing her off.

"I'm okay, Mom. I just…I just…need time," he said, sounding devastated. "Is there any more?" he hesitated as he looked at Kathy, who shook her head. "Then, may I be excused?" he asked respectfully of both women. Kathy nodded. Then, he looked down at Alice, and she looked sadly back at him for a moment before adding her nod to Kathy's. He immediately left the living room and headed for his bedroom.

Alice exchanged a look with Kathy and then, hearing a noise, whirled to see Mrs. Fernandez crying unashamedly as she listened to their conversation. She went to her and took the older woman in her arms as she cried, the first time she could ever remember such an exchange with the woman.

The Skype phone call to Kit was just as bad as they watched their eldest daughter cry unashamedly.

"Are they sure? Maybe I should come home?"

"No, darling. I want you to stay at school," Kathy told her oldest daughter. She took Alice's hand in hers and rephrased that, "We both want you to stay at school. Momma A is taking good care of me. I don't want you to lose time from your studies." Alice had her arm around Kathy and rubbed her shoulder reassuringly.

"I haven't even started. I'm still getting settled," Kit told her, gesturing to the luxurious apartment behind her that Alice had purchased. Alice bought it through an agent, who had taken her on a video tour, and she hadn't quibbled on the price as she bought it from afar for their daughter. The agent had been surprised, amazed, and pleased by turns as Alice asked questions, knowing the area from her own time at Harvard.

"How's the job?" Alice asked, trying to turn the conversation away from the cancer. The first part of the conversation had been so sad that both her wife and daughter had cried.

Kit shrugged. "It's okay," she answered, sounding nonchalant. Then she grinned, "I'm loving it, learning a lot, and making great contacts." Then she sobered. "But that isn't anything compared to what you are going through," she said, directing that last comment at Kathy.

"You don't worry about me. We're fighting this, and you have a life to live. You enjoy that job and apartment. I think Momma A overindulged you though," she said, waggling a finger at her daughter and giving Alice a look.

"*What?*" Alice asked, trying to look innocent and failing as she smiled. "She needed a place to live."

"But such a fine place?" Kathy asked, amused, as she looked through the camera of her computer and beyond her daughter to the luxurious apartment she could see.

"What?" Alice asked again. "It was a good investment."

Kit laughed at the byplay between her mothers. She was so happy to see them back together, and now, this cancer. Dammit! "Is there anything I can do?" she asked, trying to regain their attention.

"No, honey. I'll keep you apprised, but Doctor Wilkerson said I'll be going in once a week, sometimes twice a week, while we try this experimental treatment," Kathy told her, looking at her oldest earnestly.

"Twice a week? I thought cancer treatment was like once a month?"

Alice nodded as Kathy explained, "Normal treatment is once a month. This is an experimental treatment since the cancer is so aggressive and moving so rapidly. They can't wait for normal treatment, and the hope is this should halt its rapid advance."

Kit nodded as though she completely understood. "If you need...anything," she hiccupped, suddenly realizing the gravity of the situation again, "you'll call? Please?"

"I'll call every chance I get, and if I get your voicemail, I'll leave a message and let you know what's going on," Kathy promised. "I'm not going to call every day though."

Kit had been about to argue the every day comment but thought better of it. She exchanged a look with Alice, who nodded slightly. She wouldn't call every day either, but she would let Kit know if anything was amiss that Kathy didn't want to discuss.

They signed off soon afterwards, and Alice turned to Kathy. "I think you need to sleep now." She could see how exhausting this day had been for her wife.

"I concur," Kathy agreed, and they held hands as they headed for bed together.

* * * * *

Alice tried repeatedly to get through the firewall over at the Pasternack's. There was a lot she wanted to see on that woman's computer. She tried through the security company, but apparently, they too had a firewall, and it was first rate. She thought of contacting Simone in New York, who happened to own a security company too, but Alice didn't want to involve her in what she considered a family matter. It would complicate things, and things were already complicated enough.

Alice hadn't forgotten about the dear ex-senator, who still had his people regularly watching their house. She wondered why he bothered since both women knew they were there. She had relieved some stress the other night by sneaking out of the house with a handful of three-inch nails in her hand and making her way to the parked car where she propped nails up on both sides of each tire. Then, she made a 7-Eleven run for Kathy,

who said she was craving a Slurpee. Alice sped out of her driveway, taunting the men, who trying to hide in their sedan, by driving fast and too close to their vehicle. They followed for about three feet until the spikes pierced their tires. Alice returned from the store in time to see the vehicle being dragged onto a flatbed with all four of its tires flattened. She laughed. She was prepared to do it again but hadn't seen the car in a couple of days since that incident.

Alice also hadn't forgotten the hornet's nest she had stirred up in the form of Sebastian's nephew, Artum. She wished he would just let things go, but knew she had cost him quite a lot.

"Why were you talking so heatedly with the gardeners?" Kathy asked, having watched her wife through the bedroom window. She'd been taking eight of her pills and seen Alice gesturing with the lead gardener.

"Oh, I don't want those foolish palms that grow forty feet high. He must have gotten some deal on them, and he wants to plant them up here. It would be like a beacon off the cliff," she gestured to the bluffs their land abutted.

"Yeah, I don't mind the squat ones," Kathy agreed with her, gesturing to the sago palms planted around their grounds, "but those others would be an eyesore out here."

Alice felt bad lying to her wife, but it was for her own safety. "You okay? You need anything?"

"No, you go play," she smiled, referring to Alice's attempts on the computer. She'd seen some of it when Alice showed her what she had found, which wasn't much.

"I think I'm going to take a swim first and work out," Alice told her.

"Mind if I watch?" Kathy asked alluringly, laughing at her.

"You stay out of the sun. Doctor Wilkerson said that stuff will make your skin extra sensitive," she warned, referring to the chemotherapy.

Kathy watched from the safety of the overhang that protected her with its shade. She also watched as Alice played tennis with their daughter on their private court. Alice was giving instruction but wouldn't let the teen win; she had to earn it. Sean joined them, and playing against the two kids made Alice sweat, although she gave as good as she got. The three of them ended up enjoying themselves in the pool afterward. The two teens tried to entice Kathy in, but Alice explained the chlorine was not good for Kathy's skin, which was extra sensitive now. The dryness was a side effect of the chemo. One good thing that came from having dry skin was the need for lotion. Alice eagerly caressed her wife's body, massaging it while rubbing the lotion into her skin.

* * * * *

"Will you look at this?" Alice said, bringing her phone to Kathy and showing her the video playing on the screen.

"What is this?" Kathy asked, frowning as she watched what looked like a four-screen video of some security footage. She could make out four young people in the videos. They were wearing ski masks that they had pulled up on their heads, clearly showing their faces.

"The twit and her friends are robbing my house in Malibu," Alice told her angrily.

"What?" Kathy asked, alarmed, and sat up on the couch where she'd been reading the newspaper.

Alice left her phone with Kathy as she called the police on the house phone. She knew the alarm company was already on the way, but who knew how long that would take.

Kathy listened as Alice exasperatedly told the police in Malibu about the robbery in progress. She watched as they stole the television sets that had been left there to show the house, ripping the fixtures angrily from the wall. Then, with her heart in her mouth, she watched as the teens tore apart the rest of the house using the swords Alice had brought back from Kazakhstan, their razer-sharp edges making neat work of the furniture. The kids suddenly looked up and quickly exited to the beach, disappearing from the camera's view.

"Dammit!" Alice swore. The kids had not only taken the TVs and everything else of value, but also her swords. Some were seen leaving through the garage where they had loaded up a car, and the last of them were seen on the beach disappearing from view.

"Those swords are priceless," Kathy pointed out, looking up as Alice hung up the phone. "Why didn't you bring them home?"

"I forgot I'd left them when I brought the other things here, and when we put the house up for sale so quickly, I just…forgot," she finished lamely.

"You'll get them back," Kathy said confidently.

Alice looked up at her wife, who was resting on a couch in the TV room. It had taken a minute for Alice to find her when the spy cams had alerted her to intruders, and she realized what was going on at the house. Seeing who it was had instantly rekindled her age-old rage. Maybe she could not kill that *child*, but she could teach her a lesson. She thought she had already learned from her parents being financially liable for her acts, but obviously the elitist teen had not learned anything.

"I'm going to have to go into their home," she confided to her wife quietly.

"Didn't Emily say they had a security system?" Kathy worried. She sometimes liked it better when Alice did things without telling her ahead of time. She worried less that way. She wouldn't tell her wife that though. It had taken too long for them to get to the point where Alice confided with her.

"Yes, she did," Alice mused, wondering what kind of system it was since its firewall wasn't falling to her repeated attempts. It had to be a newer system, and it had to be secure because her techniques were rather...unique in their ability to thwart such systems. Her programs were state-of-the-art and illegal for the public to own...if anyone could even find them on her encrypted computers.

"How are you going to get past the security system? Are you just going in to look for the swords?" Kathy asked, confused. She was so tired, and she was starting to lose her hair. She hadn't told Alice yet, but she had seen hair on her pillow when she made the bed.

"I'm not sure. I'm going to have to scope out everything and make sure they have no night-vision cameras," she indicated her phone where the footage of the teenagers robbing her house had been clear.

"Why not just turn the kids over to the police?" Kathy asked, wanting to handle things honestly and above board for a change.

"Because the police won't get far. Sandi Pasternack will hire the best attorneys her husband's life insurance can afford, and she will get her daughter off again. That twit can't seem to grasp any of the lessons she is taught; she just amps up the ante."

"I can get you in," Emily said as she came into the room.

Both of her mothers jumped at the sound of her voice. They had been speaking low and hadn't heard her coming down the stairs.

"Dammit, Em! You have *got* to stop *eavesdropping*," Alice cursed her.

"I didn't *mean* to," she told them earnestly, looking between her moms and wondering why they wanted to get into the Pasternack's house.

Alice looked at her daughter. Just then, she looked exactly like Alice's sister Connie at the same age, and yet, when the teen grinned, she faintly reminded Alice of Kathy. She couldn't see that the child looked more like a young Alice, right down to the newly developing slant of her exotic eyes. There was also something so uniquely Em that Alice couldn't put her finger on yet.

"Those who eavesdrop never hear anything nice about themselves," Kathy said lamely, already too tired to cope with a misbehaving teen.

Alice turned to her wife with a questioning look, wondering about the sappy wisdom. Kathy grinned and shrugged. They both turned back to Emily.

"How much of that did you hear?" Alice asked.

"Something you wanted to get back from the Pasternack house?" Emily prompted, feeling a bit uncomfortable.

"You said you turned off their security system when you broke the windows," Alice began. She heard Kathy say weakly, "No, Alice," but ignored her. "Can you tell me how you did it?"

"I just punched in the code. I saw Carmen do it hundreds of times, and I guess I just learned the code from watching her."

Alice could have told her that those observation skills would come in handy. She noticed that Em was wearing sweats. She had probably been working on her karate skills in the weight room and overheard her parents talking. "What's the code?" she asked her daughter, watching her closely.

"I want to go–" began the teen, but both her parents interrupted.

"No!" Alice and Kathy said at the same time, then looked at each other and laughed.

"I don't want you getting involved in this," Kathy told her, quickly losing her smile. "This is something your mother needs to look into."

"Mom…" the teen started to protest, sounding a little bit whiny.

"Don't 'Mom' me!" Kathy answered quickly.

"Look, Em. You've already got a lot on your shoulders…" Alice began, holding up her hand to silence the teen's need to argue. "You have seen and heard some things I'd rather you hadn't. I don't want to add to that, if I can help it. I want you to have a normal life without complications."

"Come on, Mom. I can help…" she argued, despite the admonishments.

"No, you can't come with me!" Alice told her with a finality that the teen knew meant business.

"What if I don't give you the code?" Em asked saucily.

"Then, those long-awaited and long-overdue punishments will finally come to pass," Alice promised in a threatening tone that brooked no argument.

Emily stared at her parents. Kathy was looking ill, lying on the couch and holding Alice's phone. She was very pale, and against her dark hair, her skin looked even paler. Alice looked fierce. Her eyes were hard but were not changing color yet, and Emily knew better than to invoke that change. She crumbled in the face of such opposition and gave her mother the code. "What will you do?" she asked instead.

"I don't know," Alice admitted, much to the surprise of both her wife and her daughter.

"Shouldn't you have a plan?" Em asked, and Kathy turned expectantly to her wife, agreeing with the teen.

"Nope, gonna wing it," she said, smiling slightly at the amazingly similar facial expressions of her wife and daughter.

* * * * *

Alice waited a couple days; she was busy. She had to make a police report and explain what she had seen on the video, handing over the carefully doctored video of the break-in, which excluded the twit from the footage after she darkened it, so she wasn't recognizable. The others were immediately put on the police radar and would eventually be caught, but amazingly, they didn't give up their accomplice, Carmen.

Then, she took Kathy to another chemo appointment and fiddled on her phone while she waited for her to finish.

"Anything?" Kathy asked weakly from where she lay with the poison flowing into her veins. Today, it looked blue, and Alice teased her that she was now a real blue blood.

"No, I can't find what I want, and I don't dare put more of these invasive programs on a mere phone," Alice told her as she looked up, trying not to gasp at how white her wife had become. This was only the third session. She would be supportive of whatever the doctor wanted to do…until the end, and that was a real possibility. She made sure none of her thoughts showed on her face as she smiled at her wife.

"What are you looking for?" Kathy asked quietly, wondering what Alice was up to.

"I'm trying to get a handle on the senator's schedule. They've changed it three times since I tapped into their system, and I want to know why."

"The senator?" Kathy exclaimed, surprised. She had forgotten about him with all the commotion about the twit.

Alice, who had looked back down at her phone, looked up at her wife through her lashes and gave her a sardonic look in return. "You don't think I've forgotten what he has been up to, do you?"

"I thought you might, what with everything else," she gestured at the needle in her arm and thought about the other things that had occupied their attention a month ago.

Alice lowered her voice as she put the phone down and gave her wife her full attention. "I have several things I'm looking into," she confided.

"Like what?" Kathy demanded.

"We'll talk in the car," Alice hedged, not sure she wanted to share what she had found with her wife but knowing she wouldn't lie if Kathy asked a direct question, not completely anyway.

"You think someone is bugging this office?" Kathy laughed.

Alice smiled, and just then, the nurse came in to check on her patient. Alice exchanged an 'I told you so' look with her wife.

"Okay, spill," Kathy teased as they drove away from the clinic.

"Which part?" Alice muttered.

"How do you know your car isn't bugged?"

"Because I sweep it after every time I take it out."

"Every time?" Kathy asked, surprised.

"Every time," Alice admitted, glancing at her wife before concentrating on the traffic.

"Have you found anything?"

Alice shrugged and shook her head. "Not yet, but you know, it would be just my luck that one time…."

Kathy had to admit she was right. "Don't think you are going to distract me that easily. What are you watching for on your phone besides the senator?"

Alice smiled. Kathy was more insightful about her hedging these days. "Before I start, is there anywhere you want to stop before going home?"

"Wendy's?"

"Why Wendy's?" Alice asked, surprised, changing to another lane, so she could turn off and head for the chain restaurant.

"I'm craving a Wendy's chicken sandwich and baked potato. Not the spicy one though; that would give me bad heartburn," she added, rubbing her stomach. She'd suffered from a lot of heartburn with the meds she was on.

"How about a chocolate shake?" Alice enticed her.

"Sold!" Kathy answered with a smile. She knew Alice would indulge her every whim. She just hoped she wouldn't throw up all her food. It was later in the day, and she had noticed she usually threw up after breakfast and the meds she had to take early in the day. A couple of the meds required her to drink milk with them, and a couple required her to wait an hour before eating, but she always threw up after breakfast. She found if she ate a banana with some of the meds, the reflux wasn't as bad, and she could eat again. It was a horrible cycle; one the doctor had warned her about. She was also cautioned that she could easily become anemic.

Alice waited in the parking lot until Kathy was eating her chicken sandwich and digging her spoon into the chocolate Frosty she had decided to substitute for the shake. She bit into her own sandwich, a blissful look on her face as she tasted the lettuce, tomato, and fried chicken blending with the mayonnaise. "I'm trying to keep tabs on Artum and looking for Iggy. Then, there is Carmen and Sandi. I want to get in that house when

they aren't home, but neither of them is doing things on a schedule." She said it as though the pair were deliberately doing this to inconvenience her, and Kathy laughed around her food, coughing slightly as something caught, then quickly sipping at her soda.

"Careful there," Alice warned. "Not sure you want me doing the Heimlich."

"I'm okay, just tried to swallow too much," she admitted as she chewed her food finer. "Are you finding anything?"

"More than enough to hang Artum, but Iggy is still being hidden. I'm beginning to wonder if he returned to whatever hole he crawled out of, or if they killed him for stealing from our house."

"What are you going to do?"

"For now, I'm just going to watch. Things were pretty hot with Artum, and I don't want to stir that hornet's nest if I can avoid it."

"Why not?"

Alice looked at her wife incredulously. "With you sick, I don't want to jeopardize our safety."

"How would that jeopardize our safety?" she asked naively.

"He could come to our house to take revenge, and he would probably kill me," she answered succinctly.

"What about me?" Kathy asked, almost sounding hurt that she would be excluded. "I mean, I did help."

"And Emily," Alice reminded her.

"That kid is starting to worry me with everything she knows."

"Me too," Alice admitted. She'd been watching the monitors and hadn't seen anything out of the ordinary with the teen, but with all she already knew, it was a wonder Emily wasn't in therapy.

Alice finally got a break when Carmen bragged in a post that she and her mother were going to a Broadway play that had come to town. She talked about how she had purchased a gown for the event, going on and on about it. Ignoring the obvious excitement of the obnoxious teen, Alice watched the comments and the girl's responses, gleaning far more than the teen would have ever expected when she posted. The child was a font of unintentional information, and Alice waited patiently as the night in question came, planning accordingly.

She waited until Kathy had gone to bed and she thought Emily was in bed. Sean was staying at a friend's house, which he seemed to be doing a lot with Kathy looking more ill by the day. She couldn't really blame the teen. Twice by turns, he'd thought he'd lost his parents, but this time was the first time he was actually watching it happening, and it was probably deeply disturbing to him. He wasn't talking much to his parents, and Kathy and Alice were sad about that. They both hoped he was getting what he needed from his friends and their parents. Alice had carefully vetted those parents and found them and their children to be decent people, so she wasn't concerned about their influence on her son.

As she prepared on the evening of the play, she dressed carefully to conceal her blonde hair, which she kept short and spikey. She thought of blackening her face but felt that would be too hard to explain if she were caught. Using her key, she slipped out her own back gate going along the bluffs until she passed her own estate and her neighbors' before cutting back and slipping out behind the car that was watching their house tonight. Fortunately, it was not parked as close as it had been previously. Just for fun and practice, she slipped up on the car and placed three-inch nails on

both the back tires again, ensuring deep punctures and hopefully a flat tire or two when they moved. She added insult to injury by shoving a potato in the tailpipe, which made a slight noise, but the two idiots watching tonight didn't hear a thing.

It was dusk, and she picked her way onto the Pasternack estate, hoping they didn't have a dog. She didn't remember Emily stating they had one, and she thought people like Sandi and Richard, with a self-absorbed daughter like Carmen, were far too selfish to bother with pets. She thought about her own family and determined they would adopt another dog, maybe even a cat or two. It was only right that their kids have pets. She wanted them to have as normal a childhood as possible.

She determined where the motion-sensor lights were by simply triggering them, one by one, and determining their range over the course of an hour. She knew that the Pasternacks had left over an hour ago and had timed her own appearance accordingly. It wasn't so dark that she couldn't make her way to their house using her night-vision goggles and see what she needed to turn off the security system with the code Emily had given her. She feared they had changed the code and shook her head at the laziness of human nature when it worked. Richard had obviously never changed it, and Sandi probably never thought of it after his death. As she made her way into the garage, she looked around with her goggles, determined not to turn on any lights until she had to. Nothing in the garage gave her the information she was seeking, and she turned off the security alarm and made her way into the house, noting that the house wasn't particularly neat and wondering if they had a maid or housekeeper. None of her research had indicated they did. She looked through their living room, noting the dining room was the most prestigious room of the house. The kitchen needed a thorough cleaning, with dishes stacked in the

sink and on the counter. She checked through the windows into the backyard and saw no indication they had pets.

Next, she made her way upstairs to the bedrooms, realizing the master bedroom must have been the room she missed downstairs and cursing herself for thinking it was the den or office, which she was ultimately seeking. She noted that there were only two bedrooms upstairs. They were oddly narrow, and a long hallway connected both to an equally narrow shared bathroom. She checked for hidden rooms, wondering why such an oddly shaped house had been built in this expensive area of Palos Verdes. The guest room was stripped, and there was nothing to indicate it had any occupants, just a plain twin bed and desk, both bare and boring. There was nothing in the closet or under the bed as Alice's gloved fingers sought for anything hidden and dislodged some dust. She left that room and went to check out what she assumed was Carmen's room.

It looked like a tornado had hit the teen's room. The messiness she had noted downstairs was compounded by the used clothing thrown haphazardly about the room. Some clothing lying around had been folded, and she could only surmise that it had been clean at one point but never put away. The bed was unmade, the sheets were in a ball to one side, and the mattress was exposed. There were used dishes up here too, the remains of food congealed or caked on the dishes. Alice gazed at the dishes with disgust, her own fastidious nature finding the idea of attracting bugs like this abhorrent. She easily found the teen's computer. It was obviously well-used, and it was the only reasonably clean surface in the room. Alice found it still turned on and not password protected, quickly confirming her own findings that nothing was hidden. She'd installed a keylogger program through the virus the teen had experienced months ago, slowing things down until Alice could tweak it to her needs. She left the

computer, her eyes adjusting once again to the gloom before she slipped her goggles back on and searched the room. She found her swords and would have taken them, but they were listed with the police as missing, and she wasn't sure how to use this information yet. She gave the messy room a once-over but found nothing she hadn't expected and left. She froze when she saw a figure coming up the stairs.

"What in the hell are you doing here?" she hissed at Emily, recognizing her daughter, who was also dressed in black jogging clothes like Alice.

"I thought I could help," the teen stated defensively.

"Are you wearing gloves?" she asked and confirmed that the girl was not as she grabbed the handrail.

Emily looked down dumbly at her hands, realizing she was leaving fingerprints in the home. "Won't they assume they are from when I was here before?"

"Not if they are fresh. This is one of the reasons I didn't want you here; you are leaving evidence," she hissed angrily.

Emily could hear the reproach in her mother's voice and winced. She had thought she was the best person to help her mother. She wanted to witness the revenge Alice would get on these people. She hated Carmen for what she had done to her, and overhearing that her parents wanted more information on this family after Richard's death, she felt she was the best person to help them. She made as if to wipe her hand down the rail.

"Don't do that," Alice warned her. "You're making it worse by spreading your DNA all over the scene." She took her own gloved hand and wiped down the entire banister as she went down the stairs with the teen following reluctantly behind. "Don't touch anything," she ordered angrily. "What else have you touched?"

"Just the garage door you came through," she admitted honestly, thinking hard on that.

Alice sighed, wondering if she could use the teen's help or should order her home. The chances of getting caught had increased with her presence. "Did the Pasternacks have anything like video surveillance or a nanny cam or anything?" she asked, figuring she might as well use her daughter's knowledge while she could. Sending her home would only increase the chances she might be seen.

"They didn't need a nanny cam–" and Alice lifted her goggles, so she could peer through the dark and stare at her daughter as she realized the stupidity of what she was saying. "Oh..." she finished.

Alice shook her head and rolled her eyes. "Did they spy on their guests or their daughter?" she asked, heading once again for the dining room. "Don't touch *anything*," she warned.

"I don't think so." She sounded like an unsure adolescent to Alice's ears.

Alice dug in her pocket. She hadn't brought much with her, but a pair of latex gloves surfaced, and she handed them to the teen.

"Put these on and stay quiet," she ordered, watching as the teen struggled into the gloves and held up her hands to show her mother when they were on. Alice didn't approve. She had never wanted to see her teen doing something illegal. Still, she had overheard so many illegal things Alice had done, and she had observed both her parents breaking and entering, not to mention Alice eventually killing several people. The fact that she hadn't broken was amazing.

Alice pulled her goggles over her eyes again and looked around the living room and dining area once more. She was looking for telltale items that could be used to conceal a camera or holes in the walls or ceiling.

There was nothing. She'd looked before, but knowing she wasn't as quick or observant as she had once been, a second look never hurt. This time, she went into what she now knew to be the master bedroom, looking through things in the dressers, side tables, and cosmetics table the woman kept in there. She saw that Richard Pasternack's things were still in the walk-in closet. She went through everything, searching each pocket, looking but not finding anything of importance.

"What are you looking for?" Emily whispered, watching her mother for a long time, squinting through the darkness and trying to make out exactly what she was doing.

"Shhh," Alice replied, annoyed that the teen was watching her and wishing she could just send her home.

Emily subsided, but she wanted to help too. She looked around the room, peering into the darkness and wondering what Alice was looking for. She took one step towards the bed and heard her mother's voice.

"Leave it."

"What?" the teen asked, genuinely curious what Alice meant. Then, she wondered how Alice had seen her.

"Whatever it is, leave it," Alice said without even turning around.

Emily was annoyed. She wasn't eight years old anymore. She was old enough to help Alice search. She hadn't seen Alice find the sword box in Carmen's room, but if she had seen it, she wouldn't have understood Alice leaving it there. After all, Carmen had stolen it from Alice's home in Malibu. "Why can't we turn on the light or use a flashlight?" the teen asked, trying to see what Alice was fumbling for in the dark of the walk-in closet.

"Because people can see more in the light," Alice said shortly, annoyed to have to explain herself. Emily shouldn't be here. "It would give us away if we were seen through the window."

That made sense to the teen, but wouldn't it hurry things up if Alice could better see what she was looking for? "I brought along a penlight, and it should…" the teen began, fumbling with the light that she turned on in her hand.

Alice turned slightly, just in time to have the light flashed in her eyes. "Dammit!" she exclaimed, closing her eyes to its glare, which was magnified by the goggles she was wearing. "Turn that damned thing off!" she hissed at her daughter, angry now. "You've blinded me!"

"Sorry," Emily said quickly and scrabbled to turn off the small light, wondering why something so small could have her mother sounding so angry.

Alice recalled giving her daughter the penlight. It was cheap but effective, and now. she was blinded. She rapidly blinked away the white spots before her eyes. She sighed. She wished her daughter had stayed home, so this would go faster. She'd already been here too long and hadn't even looked through the office yet. She wasn't finding much here in the bedroom, and she had to be careful to put everything back exactly as she found it, so no one would be aware that she had rifled through their things.

She finally headed out of the bedroom and into the master bathroom, looking around at the opulence. It was rather nauseating and overboard; it bespoke of wealth…without class. Everything was gold-plated: the faucets, the edges of the mirrors, and even the toilet and bidet. It was over the top and gaudy, and it reminded Alice of pictures she had seen of other wealthy people who seemed to think that having gold on everything

showed their wealth off splendidly. It didn't. There was no taste shown here at all. She found Sandi Pasternack had a taste for expensive name brand perfumes. They were overpriced and not nearly as fine as the ones Alice and Kathy used, which were custom made for them by Alice's perfumer. This woman had all the finest, top brand cosmetics, but extraordinarily little of the products was used. Alice finally saw the first thing that had her narrowing her cat-like eyes. She realized that all the fine cosmetics were there for show only. Behind the cosmetics was a false door, and Alice carefully opened it.

"Give me your penlight," Alice whispered to her daughter, pulling off her goggles with one hand and holding out her other hand expectantly.

"What'd you find?" the teen whispered back, suddenly excited.

"Never mind," Alice murmured, taking the light her daughter handed her and glancing around the glass-enclosed bathroom once she had turned it on. She aimed its beam into the drawer as she shielded the beam with her hand to keep it from flashing outside the box. She tugged slightly at the false door, pulling it open to reveal syringes and several vials. Her eyes narrowed at the Russian lettering, trying to wrack her brain and remember what Sasha had taught her so long ago. She couldn't make out what the substances were, but they all seemed to be the same. She slipped one into her pocket and carefully closed the hidden door, piling the makeup against it, then opening and shutting the drawer a couple of times to hide where she had been from her daughter.

"What is that?" Emily asked, curious.

"I don't know," Alice admitted, turning off the penlight and handing it back to her daughter. She thought about keeping the penlight but didn't want to encumber herself with anything in case she needed her hands free, and she had limited pocket space. Her jogging clothes weren't built for

carrying much, and the bulge of the little glass vial was patently obvious to her. She grabbed the goggles again and looked around the bathroom some more, feeling under the sink cabinet for hidden spaces and anything else that Sandi or Richard might have reason to hide. Then she got up, hearing her knees crack with the effort as she headed for the office. She knew she should have gone there first but had relished the idea of leaving it for last. She would give it a thorough go-through and then leave, but with Emily along and watching, she would have to see what she could do despite the teen. She sighed at the inconvenience.

The office, or rather a den-like room, was the complete opposite of the display of wealth that had been so obvious in the master bedroom. This room was warm with dark woods that Alice could appreciate, but it also told her that Richard Pasternack had taste and his wife did not. The dark wood made it harder to discern if there were hidey-holes as it hid any telltale signs. She wished for a light but knew that would be a mistake of the highest order and could give away their presence completely. The shelf-lined walls held books in several languages, and her minimal knowledge of Russian proved useful as she realized they were versions of books like The Art of War by Sun Tzu and other classics: from Shakespeare in Russian to what she gleaned were The Harry Potter books, not in Russian but what she figured out was a similar language. With a name like Pasternack, she thought perhaps they were Ukrainian? She didn't know and would have to look into that another time. After looking over the various titles—few, if any, in English—for telltale signs of hidey-holes, she heard her daughter whisper.

"What are we looking for?" Emily was becoming impatient and bored. Whatever she had thought they would find and investigate, it wasn't Mr.

Pasternack's collection of first editions or leather-bound, stinky books. Some of them were ancient, and she'd seen them all before.

"I won't know until I find it, will I?" Alice answered, amused. "You weren't supposed to be here, so be quiet and let me look," she admonished in a warning tone.

Emily subsided, chastised and annoyed. She wanted to help. After all, she was the one that had the code to the house, so why couldn't she… She took a step towards the desk and heard Alice speak without even turning around.

"Touch nothing. Just stand there," she told the girl.

"Why can't I help?"

"What are we looking for?" Alice countered, seeing something out of the ordinary and reaching for two books that had obviously been pulled out recently, if the telltale signs in the dust were correct.

"I don't know," the teen admitted and wondered if her mother was going to sit down and read as she reached for some books.

Alice was glad she was wearing gloves; her fingerprints would be obvious on these books since they were so smooth. The covers weren't leather though; they were some other material. As she opened the first book, she realized the two books were bonded together as one, and when she opened them to the center, it revealed a small box. She carefully put the books down on a side table, moving aside a large mound of paperwork to accommodate them. She pulled the box out but was unable to open it. It didn't have any signs of a lock, or even a hinge, and she studied it carefully.

"What is it?" Emily asked, unable to control herself.

"I think it's some sort of safe or something," Alice murmured, mostly to herself as she examined it. It was then she realized that some of the

pages were thicker than others and moved. "Bring your light here but cover it with your hands," she ordered her daughter as she lifted the goggles to her head to peer into the darkness.

"Hey, that's cool," Em told her as she shined her penlight on the book that wasn't a book.

"Were you any good at Rubik's Cubes?" Alice asked her daughter, realizing there had to be a pattern to the page squares carved in the sides of the books.

"Wasn't that a Russian game?" Emily asked as she reached for the books, handing Alice the penlight, so she could touch the odd squares carved into the sides of the pages. It wasn't as easy as it would have been with bare hands, but she knew better than to take off the gloves.

"You should know that it was developed by a Hungarian," she corrected her daughter as she watched, amazed, as Emily adeptly pushed and prodded the cubes into place. They slid easily under her fingertips, or so it appeared to Alice's eyes.

Emily shrugged as she studied the cube and began to place her fingers on the thick slips of paper. "I just remember the craze; it wasn't very easy to get the nine squares on all the sides to match."

"You should learn the history of things too; that does become important," Alice advised, watching fascinated as her daughter figured out the complex slides that looked too complicated to her. Then, she too saw the pattern and pointed out a couple moves to her daughter, "Move that one there, and go up there," she advised, and the book suddenly released the box from its interior with a ping.

"Whoa!" Emily exclaimed rather loudly.

"Shhh," Alice told her as she reached for the box, which contained several wads of cash in both US dollars and English pounds. It was at the bottom of this small box that she found data sticks; those she took out.

"Aren't you going to take the money?" Emily asked, surprised.

Alice shrugged. "Why? I have enough," she answered as she put the money back and closed the box, quickly mixing up the sliders to hide the combination once again. She wiped the sides where Emily had touched the book, despite the fact she was wearing gloves, hoping that no one would notice it had been opened. Hearing a noise, she turned out the light, closed the books, and slid her goggles back on while returning the books to their shelf. She waited a while, listening to her daughter's breathing in the dark.

"What was that?" Emily asked quietly, barely getting the words out.

"I don't know," Alice admitted as she slid the books carefully back onto the shelf and looked towards the computer. Removing something from her pocket she replaced it with the data sticks.

"What's that?"

"Shhh," Alice told her as she carefully put some pea-sized cameras on the shelves, trying not to disturb any of the dust that had built up and leave any signs of their presence. Just as she was placing the second one, she caught her daughter's hand before she could touch the shelf. "No," she said quietly. "You'll leave evidence."

Emily hadn't thought of that. She'd been about to put her hand on the shelf as she tried to see what her mother was doing. She realized Alice must be quite good at this. She seemed to effortlessly examine things, and Emily had no idea how she saw things. She would have totally missed those books.

Alice next moved to the desk and began to rifle through the drawers, being sure to feel on the upper parts of the various inserts for hidden or concealed spots. In the last and biggest drawer, which was filled with paperwork she could not read in the dark, she found another data stick, and she slipped this in with the others.

"Why is that one blue?" Emily asked softly, noting the others had all been white.

"No idea," Alice admitted, shrugging but also a little pleased her daughter had also noticed the difference. Finally, Alice reached for the computer to turn it on. The computer was old, and the light from the screen was rather bright. Alice slipped her goggles onto her head and hoped that the glare and reflection on the window wouldn't give them away. She almost said something as Emily moved to the window and closed the drapes, then thought better of it.

A password prompt came up, but Alice had been prepared for it as she put her own stick into a USB port. The software rapidly scrolled through various combinations until it found the password. "Not too obvious," Alice murmured sarcastically as she realized the password was Pasternack, their last name. She took another data stick from her pocket and replaced the password stick in the port. She began to download everything from the computer onto it.

"Will there be enough room?" Em asked, watching Alice.

"I have no idea," she admitted as she began clicking on the history. The Pasternacks must have thought themselves smart as she found their banking information from several banks, smiling to herself at how easy they had made it by storing their passwords on the computer. Didn't they know you should *never* store passwords for financial information? She copied the links, then went to the password list and began copying those as

well. What Alice was doing was second nature to her, and while she was thinking she remembered something she had wanted to check for in the house, but Em had distracted her. Before turning off the computer, she installed a keylogger program she had paid a lot of money for. It was so sophisticated that it wouldn't be detected without special equipment or programs. "Open the drapes. Leave them the way they were," she informed the teen as she looked about the desk, ensuring it was the same as when she started.

"Are we done?" Emily asked after she had reopened the drapes and peered out. It was too dark to see anything.

"You should be," Alice murmured, annoyed that she was answering to a teenager. She had to think beyond her own safety now, and it was causing her to slow down. She should have already been out of the house. "I have to check one more thing," she said as she looked around the library a final time, putting her goggles on to peer through the dark.

"What?" the teen asked, curious, as she followed Alice.

"Just stay quiet," Alice stated as she headed to the master bedroom again and began peering around.

Em ignored the mandate and asked, "What are you looking for?"

Alice sighed through her nose, exasperated at the teen's questions. "I'll know when I find it. Now, be quiet," she ordered.

Em subsided, wishing somehow, some way, she could help.

Alice began to look through the jewelry. She could recognize fine pieces, but most of this was fake, cosmetic, and gaudy. The woman's taste was not Alice's. "Do you know if they had a safe?" she asked the teen, then turned when Emily didn't immediately answer. She looked questioningly at her daughter.

Emily peered at her in the darkness, barely able to make out what Alice was doing, much less seeing. Then, seeing her mother's questioning look, she answered peevishly, "You told me to be quiet."

Alice sighed. "Now is not the time for hurt feelings or dramatics. Since you are here, help me. I didn't want you here; I didn't want you involved in any of this," her hands gestured around the house they had been searching.

"But I can help," the teen contended.

"You have helped. Now, answer my question. Did they have a safe?"

"I don't remember," she admitted. "What are you looking for?"

"A ring," she murmured as she turned back to the jewelry box, itself a cheap imitation wood, and rifled through things. "Mrs. Pasternack wore a ring the day we signed the paperwork in the lawyer's office, and I want to find it."

"Do you remember what it looked like?" Em asked reasonably, suddenly happy she might be able to help.

"No. Unfortunately, I wasn't looking at it in the office," she admitted, annoyed at herself. That wasn't like her. Normally, she was very observant. She closed her eyes for a moment to try to pinpoint that moment in time, to remember and focus. It took her a moment to get there, and she had to shush Emily once more as she concentrated. "I think it was like a signet ring. You know, one of those rings you wear when you graduate from high school or college?" she said to the teen. "She had turned it around," she said, remembering the incident now that she concentrated, and using her unique mind, she began to play it out. "Do you remember seeing anything like that?"

"Why would she turn it around?" the teen asked, confused, as she tried to remember ever seeing a ring anything like that on her friend's mother.

Alice was getting exasperated. She wasn't finding it as she rifled through the crap jewelry while trying not to get anything out of place. They were running out of time. "Because I think it has a needle in it, and she used it to hurt your mom!"

Emily drew back, horrified. She wasn't stupid, and her young, agile mind began to put the pieces of the puzzle together. "Do you think she made mom sick with whatever was in that needle?"

Alice immediately regretted becoming annoyed with her daughter. The goggles clearly showed Emily's face in the dark. "Yes, I do," she admitted honestly, calming her voice and putting the jewelry box back. She wanted to take Em in her arms and comfort her, but now was not the time or the place. They had to get out of here. "I think we're going to have to leave it for another time," she admitted as she went to the side table and looked through it again.

Emily was deeply horrified by what she had learned. If that were true, then Mrs. Pasternack had poisoned her mom! She looked around the dark room, trying to remember what she had seen during the times she had been here. She had no reason to come in here but had followed her friend when she came to borrow something. Mrs. Pasternack certainly wasn't as neat as her own mothers. "What about her medical bag?" she whispered to Alice, who turned around quickly.

"Where is it?" she asked, suddenly interested.

"She usually keeps it in the garage."

Alice returned the items she had rifled in the side table exactly where she had found them and closed the drawer. "Let's go," she said to the teen. The garage was on their way out. "What does it look like?" she asked as they headed for the door.

"Just one of those doctor's bags you see on all the old TV shows."

Alice nodded, unsure whether her daughter saw her or not as she gently opened the thick door. Looking around the three-car garage, she saw the vehicles that the Pasternacks drove, minus the one they must be using tonight. Along one side of the garage were shelving units with all sorts of junk piled on them. This must be Sandi's domain because everything was a real mess. Near the empty spot in the garage, there was one shelving unit that contained nursing items: masks, gloves, bandages, and a host of things that had Alice narrowing her eyes. She was wondering if they were stolen from the woman's employers or if she kept a supply of her own. The bag that Em had mentioned was sitting there in plain sight—at least plain sight through the goggles although outlined in green—and Alice eagerly reached for it, opening it and trying to peer into the black depths.

"Want my penlight?" Em breathed, staying close to Alice since she could barely see in the darkness.

"Yeah, but make sure you don't shine it anywhere near the door," Alice nodded as the teen flicked the penlight on and shone it in the bag, making sure her back was towards the door and the side yard out of the garage. The door had a big window in its center.

The bag was filled with syringes, meds, bandages, and other paraphernalia. Alice was careful as some of the syringes did not have caps. It proved that Sandi was not a very conscientious nurse.

"Jeeze," Emily said, sounding impressed and repulsed. She could see blood on some of the syringes.

Alice went very carefully, making sure she didn't get stuck as she rifled through the mess. At the bottom she found the ring she was looking for, and using a plastic bag from Sandi's own supplies, she dropped the ring inside and pocketed both.

"That's it?" Emily asked as she watched her mother.

"Yeah, let's get out of here and reset the alarm," Alice told her, sensing the teen felt the end was anti-climactic. They put the medical bag back on the shelf once Alice closed it up and headed for the alarm panel. Alice reset it with Emily's help, and they headed for the side door to make their escape. They put the code in just in time. Right then, the garage light came on, blinding Alice with its brilliance as it shone through her goggles. They both heard the garage door rising.

"Come on!" Emily gasped, realizing Alice couldn't see as she fumbled for the doorknob. Em grabbed her mother's arm and yanked her out the door into the dark just as the garage door rose completely.

"Shit!" Alice swore angrily, blinking rapidly to remove the spots from her eyes.

They headed for the path that wound down both sides of the road, the jogging path running behind the houses on Alice and Kathy's side of the block along the bluff. As they darted across the road, behind the car eternally parked there, they both looked back. Alice lifted her goggles to blink blindly in the dark at the house they had just left.

"Can you see anything?" Alice whispered, still unable to get rid of the spots. The light from the garage had gone right through the night goggles.

"Yeah, it's Mrs. Pasternack. I can't see anyone else," Emily whispered, sounding excited.

"Just get me home," Alice warned her. She didn't need to be caught now.

Emily led her along the bluff, noting that Alice was still having trouble. They were almost to their own gate when Alice finally freed her arm from Emily's grip. "Thanks," she murmured as she unlocked the gate, and they both went through. Alice relocked it with the key, and they crossed their lawn and entered the house.

"Where have you been?" Kathy rasped, looking at them both in consternation as they came into the kitchen together.

Alice looked up, surprised. Kathy had known where she was going, but she looked guiltily at her daughter standing beside her. Alice realized how that looked when Kathy asked, "You took Emily *with* you?"

"No, I–" she began, but Em interrupted.

"No, I followed her. I thought I could help," she admitted, looking as chastised and guilty as Alice felt. She bit her lip and leaned from foot to foot uncomfortably.

"You *followed* your mom?" Kathy asked, incredulous. She'd known Alice a lot of years, and that wouldn't have been possible in the past. She looked between the two faces to see if they were lying to her.

"Yeah, I know. I'm in trouble," the teen said, sounding rebuked.

"Do you know what would have happened if I had been caught?" Alice asked, putting her goggles down on the table. "And what if you had been caught?"

"What would happen?" Emily asked reasonably, her curiosity piqued.

"I don't think Portia could have gotten you out of the system," she answered ominously. "I probably would have gone to jail for trespassing, breaking and entering, and who knows what else."

"And they would have been on to us for finding out about their habits," Kathy added. She looked at her wife, feeling like she was about to throw up again. She'd spent an uncomfortable night trying to keep her meds down while wondering how Alice was faring. She asked, "Did you find anything?"

"I don't know yet, but we will see," Alice told her honestly, hoping her daughter wouldn't talk too much, or not at all.

Sensing that Alice didn't want Kathy to know what they found, the teen kept quiet. She didn't want to find out how much trouble she was in by reminding them of her presence.

"You aren't to speak about this night's escapade," Alice cautioned her daughter. "You might want to go to bed while I discuss things with your mom. And you are not to eavesdrop. Do you hear me?" she warned her ominously.

"I wasn't–" she began, then shut up. She knew she'd overheard and seen some things she shouldn't have, just enough that she wanted to know more. Wisely, she knew that now was not the time, so she backed down. "Yes, Mom. Good night, Mom," she said, leaning over to give Alice a peck on the cheek and taking a step to give Kathy one as well.

"Good night, darling," Kathy murmured weakly. She could feel her stomach roiling, realizing her daughter had probably experienced something she shouldn't have.

They both waited until they heard the teen's bedroom door close.

Kathy rounded on Alice. "Why didn't you bring her right home?"

"I didn't know she was there until I was about halfway through my search. That little twit kept my swords," she informed her wife, changing the subject.

"I don't care–" began Kathy, but a coughing fit cut her off as her throat was choking up from the bile. She went into the kitchen to get a glass of water with Alice following.

"Is there anything I can get you?" Alice asked, worried about that cough.

Kathy shook her head and waved her away.

Alice stood there weakly, not knowing what she could do for her wife. She wasn't as unobservant as Kathy would like her to be. She could see

the bald patches where her hair was coming out in gobs. She had heard the choking coughs in the bathroom, the sound of her wife throwing up daily after she took her meds, and the repeated toilet flushing as her wife couldn't keep anything in or down from either end. She also could smell the severe diarrhea, and Alice had dutifully reported everything to the doctor.

Kathy continued to wave Alice away as she drank water and turned her back on her wife. She needed to cope with this part of her illness by herself.

Defeated, Alice went upstairs to change for bed, hiding the vial and the ring where she could access them tomorrow, then heading downstairs to her computers with the data sticks. Kathy found her there about an hour later.

"Anything?" she asked as she walked in carrying a large cup of water and eating salted crackers from a bag. She acted as though nothing had happened.

"That woman is pure evil," Alice commented as her computers went over the various sticks she had taken as well as the information she had downloaded.

"What about Richard?" she asked, curious. After all, he had confessed and was washing money for those drug dealers.

Alice shook her head. "It seems that Sandi is the brains of that outfit. She loved Dick," she grinned as she said that, referring to Richard. "He was only the accountant, but damn," she whistled, "he knew how to hide it." Alice showed the trail of how Richard had taken the drug money and funneled it through various enterprises ranging from fast food restaurants to some of the hospice care homes that Sandi worked in.

"What do you mean Sandi is the brains?" Kathy asked. That sounded odd to her.

"She directed where he worked and apparently, for whom. Sebastian was bad, don't get me wrong, but whoever his nephew is, or was back in the old country, he's brought an element in that I don't like," she waved to her computer screen. "That woman! I have to wonder if she's related to any of the people I met back in Mother Russia," she added, lowering her voice, so the children wouldn't hear if any were still awake.

"Sean is over at a friend's house," Kathy told her, reminding her that he spent a lot of time away. He couldn't cope with seeing Kathy looking the way she did. "I checked on Em, and she's asleep."

"Are you sure?" Alice asked. She'd checked too and wasn't so sure about that at the time.

"Yeah, this time I went in and stood there a while. There is no way she could have faked it that long," Kathy laughed. They both knew they had a handful in their teenaged daughter. She knew too much and was too strong headed. "What are we going to do with her?"

"I don't know," Alice admitted. There was just so much they could do. The teen really could hold what she knew over them, but at the same time, if she ever leaked what she knew, they were all in a lot of trouble. "We'll let my programs finish this up and go to bed. I'm tired," she admitted, stretching.

Kathy was pleased to see Alice get up and walk over to her, then take her in her arms and give her a hug and a squeeze. "We'll figure this out," Alice promised as she escorted her wife to bed.

* * * * *

Alice got up early, not needing as much sleep as her wife. She watched as Em headed off for summer camp where she was taking tennis lessons with some of her friends. She was relieved to have the girl out of the house, so she could work on her computers and go through the vast amounts of information the thumb drives contained. These sticks of information were invaluable. They told her things about Sebastian's vast network, which was now his nephew's. She hadn't known they were under so many different holdings, and she needed this information. She was sending out inquiries and waiting to read more of the information when Kathy came down the stairs.

"Are you going with me to the doctor's today?" she asked, sounding exhausted and looking pale and drawn.

"Yes. Is it at ten or eleven?" she asked to confirm.

"Eleven. We can pick up lunch afterwards?"

"Sounds good. I'll just finish up here," she indicated the computers she had cued up. She'd already pressed buttons to hide what was really on her screens, even from her wife. It was a long-standing habit of hers that she just couldn't let go of, even after all these years.

* * * * *

Doctor Wilkerson was pleased to get the vial. Even though he couldn't read the label, he was going to run some tests to find out what it was. He was even more amazed at the ring Alice handed him in the plastic baggie. When Alice showed him the needle in the false front of the ring, his eyes glimmered. He looked at it under a microscope and saw dried blood on its tip.

"I'll get right on this," he said.

"I want to know if that's Kathy's blood on there," Alice told him forcefully. "I also want to know if that's what caused this odd cancer in her body, if there is a cure, and if so, what that cure is," she indicated the vial.

"Of course," he assured her, wanting to get on that immediately, but he had to finish Kathy's treatment first.

Kathy was coughing from the lack of oxygen in her system, and Doctor Wilkerson quickly cued up the pure oxygen and put the mask on her face. Smiling kindly, he explained why her body was reacting the way it was.

Kathy remembered meeting him many years ago when she had wanted children, and Alice had arranged it for them. She still didn't understand how it was possible for two women to have children who looked like both of them, but she trusted this kind man. He was brilliant, and he had come through for them several times. She only hoped he could come through this time. She wanted to be here for her children. Hell, she wanted to be here for her grandchildren.

* * * * *

Alice kept her promise and took Kathy to her favorite fast-food restaurant after her treatment.

"If I tell you to pull over, pull over quickly!" Kathy warned after eating her hamburger and fries. It all tasted so good going down.

"Why?" Alice asked before thinking.

"Because I don't know how long that food is going to stay down, and I don't want to throw up in your nice SUV," she informed her wife as she sipped her soda, relishing the burps it produced.

Alice felt bad. She should have realized why without Kathy having to explain. She took her wife home; glad she didn't have to throw up but concerned as Kathy weakly made her way upstairs to take a nap.

Alice went downstairs to resume her study of the information she had stolen. There was just so much of it to sort through, and her eyes narrowed as she realized the enormity of it all and how she could use it.

Kathy got up later in the day when she heard Sean and Emily come in and head for the kitchen. While buttoning a new blouse, she saw Alice talking intently with a couple of the gardeners and wondered what that was about. The new gardeners had been doing a terrific job and were much better than the crew they'd had before the authorities dug up the yard. She wondered what had instigated the conversation they were now having.

* * * * *

One by one, the large, black Suburbans pulled up in front of the CIA building. There were ten in all. Four men and women got out of each one and headed for the front doors. Each was holding their identification badges in hand for security. Their presence overwhelmed security, and a button was pushed, but not before several of them got through and headed for the elevators, filling the first car as they headed upstairs.

Madelyn Korbel was notified of their impending presence before they reached the conference room where she was working with her team. Director Wolf was hurrying from his offices after getting off the emergency phone call he had just taken. By the time he arrived in the conference room, the first batch of agents, all wearing FBI windbreakers, had reached the conference room.

"Who is in charge here?" an authoritative voice asked as they entered.

"I am," Madelyn and Director Wolf responded simultaneously. They looked at each other, an understanding passing between them, and faced the blue-jacketed men and women, presenting a united front.

"We're here to gather all evidence on one Alice Weaver."

"You can't do that," several voices rang out, but Madelyn silenced her people with a simple wave of the hand.

"What's this about?" she asked, glancing at Director Wolf.

"All domestic information on Alice Weaver is to be turned over to the FBI," he told her, his expression warning her not to argue.

"ALL information," the man in charge of the agents spoke as even more agents were arriving behind him.

Wolf faced the man squarely, challenging him. "I'm sorry, some of the information is beyond your pay grade and will not be leaving this building."

The man made to interrupt, but Wolf continued, "Some of the information was received from international sources and will not be released unless I say so. As I wasn't asked beforehand about a cooperative sharing of the information, which we had been doing with the FBI–" he began, but the man had worked up enough courage to interrupt the director.

"You kept firing our agents and relieving them of their duty here–"

"Because they couldn't keep an open mind, and some of them–" began Madelyn, alarmed as several agents began to edge out around her own. She signaled her own people to begin covering up the boxes of information they had compiled, and a couple turned over the top pages on the piles of paperwork that were stacked all over the conference table.

"Ms. Korbel, I'm very well aware of the pissing match you have gotten into with several of our agents–" began the man.

"This isn't about that," Wolf interjected, "and if you're going to use that kind of language, I'm going to toss you out, then you'll have to get a court order for the information to be shared."

"Oh, *excuse me*," he stated in a sarcastic voice, glancing at Madelyn and the other women present. "I didn't realize you had sugar ears."

"Look, you gave us no notice you wanted to take over all the domestic aspects of this highly complicated case," Wolf interjected again. "So, if you give us a few hours I'm certain we can–"

"I'm here now, and I expect to take these boxes of information with us," he signaled his men and women, many who had arrived during the conversation.

"Take one step farther…" Director Wolf threatened, and the FBI agents all heard the cocking of shotguns behind them, not having noticed the large presence of CIA security that had followed them up.

The FBI agent in charge backed down immediately. "We'll wait here while you sort this…." His hands indicated the large piles of information on the conference table. He wasn't a stupid man—stubborn, yes, stupid, no.

Madelyn exchanged a look with Director Wolf, and he nodded slightly. She quickly began to give orders to her people, asking them to call in their assistants, who were assigned with helping to sort out the piles and fetch more boxes. It took hours, and the FBI agents fidgeted as they waited. So many pieces of paper and so many piles and boxes that weren't given to them, which made them itchy to see what they contained. No one left the room except the assistants as they fetched coffee, paperwork, copies, and boxes. Slowly, the day went by as the standoff continued. The CIA security all stood at attention, looking over the heads of the FBI agents while the information was sorted, boxed, and stacked. Finally, Madelyn

began nodding to Wolf that the agents could take the boxes they had separated. When the last box of paperwork was gone from the room, and the FBI agents had left with security following them out to the now loaded Suburbans, she and several others sat down with long overdue sighs. Madelyn got back up with a gesture from Wolf and followed him back to his private office.

"What the hell was that all about?" she asked once he had closed the door behind her.

"Someone has been investigating Alice Weaver and realized that the FBI didn't have all the data they felt they should have. As you weren't sharing as much as they felt you should, all domestic information about her has been returned entirely to the FBI." He held up a hand to silence her arguments. He already knew them himself. "You will continue working on the information that she provided us for the international aspects. That's a CIA prerogative," he smiled wryly. "I hope most of what you gave them," his thumb pointed to the cars that had left their drive rather abruptly, "were copies?"

Madelyn nodded and asked, "Who is creating such a hard line of authority between the agencies? We were cooperating with them."

He shrugged slightly. "I only got the order about three minutes before they arrived at our doors. Some really important senators are pissed that the CIA overstepped their authority and was handling *a domestic case*, as they saw it."

"It crossed over," she pointed out, and he nodded.

"Yes, it did, and someone in power got their knickers in a knot," he mused, wondering who. "Let's get the information we need on the money trail and earn our paychecks, okay?"

Madelyn nodded. She knew if someone in the senate oversight committee or some other powerful senator or congressman/woman was behind this, they could make things extremely difficult for them. A lot of what they did was, by necessity, secretive. Hell, she had so many balls in the air, and juggling was just a small part of that. That they specifically wanted Alice Weaver's files made her very suspicious.

"You know, we are going to need something more from Alice eventually," he pointed out, not for the first time.

"Yes, I know," she sighed, wondering how she was going to get it. Alice Weaver wasn't known for her cooperation.

* * * * *

Alice was back at her computers before dinner when Emily came tripping down the steps, sounding every bit like the teen she was.

"Hey, Mom. Anything I can do to help?"

Alice looked up at her, and for a second, she saw her sister in the young face. It startled her. The eyes weren't quite hers though. They weren't her sister's either, and they certainly weren't Kathy's. Her eyes were reminding Alice more of a predator of sorts as she grew into the young woman she would be someday. Right now, she was just too…coltish. "No, and I want you to forget about doing *anything* to help anymore. We could have gotten into a heap of trouble last night, and your mom would never have forgiven me."

"She worries too much," the teen stated with the absolute conviction of youth.

"Your mother loves you very much and doesn't want to see you get hurt," Alice countered, pressing a button as the teen tried to walk

nonchalantly behind the desk and see what her mother was reading. The screens changed, each displaying a different scene, but nothing that would give away what she had been scanning. To the viewer, one looked like stocks with the ticker tape rolling across the screen, another showed a news report, and yet another screen saver displayed scenes of Africa. It was an old trick; one she had used on Kit many times after she had come to live with them so long ago.

"Aww, Mom. Why can't I see?" she asked, realizing what Alice had done.

"Because I don't want you involved," Alice told her reasonably. "Now, go up and help your mom make dinner. I'm starving, and Mrs. Fernandez has the night off."

"Bet Sean wouldn't have had to help," she mumbled as she stomped off.

"Wait. Isn't he home?" Alice asked. She hadn't known her son wasn't home yet.

"No, he asked Mom if it was okay if he borrowed the Rav4. He said you told him it was okay?"

Alice hadn't said it was; she hadn't even seen her son when he got home from his friend's house. That would have to stop. She got up. "I'll help you make dinner," she said impulsively, annoyed that she had assumed Kathy, who was so sick, would make them dinner. How selfish of her. She'd have to make sure Kathy was better taken care of. She felt so helpless.

Kathy was surprised when she came downstairs and Alice was taking pan-fried steaks out and removing baked potatoes from the oven. The green beans made a great accompaniment, and she was pleased she was able to eat it all. Even better, everything seemed to be staying down.

Alice waited until she and Em had cleared the table, rinsed the dishes, stacked them in the dishwasher, and set the dishwasher to auto start before she sent the teen off to watch some TV. "Did Sean tell you I said it was okay for him to take the Rav4?" she asked casually as she pretended to wipe down the last of the clean counter.

"Yes. Didn't you?" Kathy asked, looking up at her wife.

Alice shook her head and tried not to smile at the trick their son had played on them. He didn't manipulate them often, but when he tried, they always caught him. He was normally an honest kid.

"Why that…" Kathy began, but her own grin belied her anger.

Alice was laughing at the incident when she caught a glimpse of someone coming over one of their fences.

"Kathy," she warned. "Go upstairs and grab an emergency bag for yourself. Get Em to take one too. You only have a few minutes." Her face fell at that moment when she observed the gardeners challenging the intruder, and she insisted, "Kathy, go! Take Em and go."

"What? Where?" she asked, concerned. "Alice, I need to help," she said, trying to make her wishes known as she rose, alarmed, and tried to see what Alice had seen.

"They are coming here. They are gonna trash the house," Alice said calmly, much more calmly than she felt. She looked up when she saw Em coming into the kitchen. "You! Go pack a bag. Enough for a week. Give me your phone," she said, holding out her hand.

"What?!" Em asked in consternation, holding onto her link with the world for all it was worth.

"You heard me. Now." She made a come-hither motion with her fingers. "Give me your phones NOW!" She indicated Kathy's as well.

"Alice," Kathy said warningly.

"No, Kathy. They are going to realize and come for us. Take her to the valley. You are not to go out." She held out her hand, and she looked so fierce they both complied, dropping the smart phones into her hand. Alice dropped the phones on the counter, putting her own next to them. Looking at her kid, she softened her face as she said, "Go upstairs and pack quickly. Do not call your friends, and don't even think of going on the computer." Kathy and Em had their backs to the kitchen window and didn't see that another person had jumped the fence and one of the gardeners had taken him down.

Emily immediately looked guilty, her thoughts betraying her. "But where–?" she began.

"Look, the family is in danger," Alice told her, grasping her shoulders and wanting to shake the teen into complying. "Those guys that looted our house are coming back. Remember how much we replaced around here," she gestured towards her computers downstairs but also towards the shelves where some of their knickknacks resided. "Please, do what your mom tells you," she indicated Kathy, who was looking concerned.

Kathy and Emily exchanged looks, scrutinized the deadly-calm-looking Alice, and headed quickly for the stairs.

"Alice–" Kathy began, but Alice put her finger over her mouth. She called out loudly, "Get packed. I won't warn you again!" They both heard Emily hurrying up the stairs. Alice took her finger off Kathy's mouth and said more softly, "You know this is necessary. Maybe they won't trash the house, but I want to keep you and the kids safe."

"I want to take the fight to them. That's what you are going to do, aren't you?" she asked.

Alice never changed expression, so Kathy wasn't certain.

"I need to help you with this," the brunette pleaded. "It's Artum, isn't it?"

"How can you help me?" Alice asked her reasonably, nimbly sidestepping the question. "I need someone to take care of the children. We have to–" she began, but Kathy interrupted her.

"They are my family too," she reminded her wife, looking at her fiercely.

"But what if something happens to us?" Alice asked.

"Alice, you know I love you. You know I love our kids, right?" At Alice's slight nod she continued, "I need to know I can protect them too."

"How are we going to keep them safe? With you there sitting on them…" she began, again trying to reason with her wife. "We can pick Sean up on the way."

"You don't think they'll listen?"

Alice gave her a look that had them both shaking their heads. No, their kids wouldn't stay put without supervision.

"Is there enough time?" Kathy asked, hearing noises from outside for the first time and turning to look. She was horrified to see several men jumping the fence and the gardeners apparently taking them down. "Alice, what…?" she began.

"Come on, there is no time. Physical objects can be replaced," Alice told her. "There is no more time. Get to the car, and I'll join you," she promised. She raised her voice and called, "Emily! Now! Come help your mother."

"But where are you–?" Kathy asked as Alice sprinted for the steps to the office.

"Just a backup on the computers. No worries," she said over her shoulder as she went. She'd been sloppy. If any of those men found those

sticks, they would take them to Artum, and she couldn't have that. She needed bargaining space, and she wasn't sure how long the gardeners could hold the men off. She quickly executed a couple keystrokes and swiped the sticks off her desk, counting them as she slipped them into the safe. She set the traps and closed it up. Quickly, she headed back upstairs.

"Come on!" she said as she found her wife and daughter at the garage door. They'd wasted too much time as it was.

"What about my meds?" Kathy asked suddenly, alarmed.

"There's no time," Alice told her, pushing her towards the Rover.

"Alice, if we're gone for any length of time…."

Alice hesitated only a moment before turning and sprinting through the house and up the stairs. She ran into the master bedroom and into the bathroom. Seeing the line of pill bottles on the windowsill, she scooped them up. She saw more on Kathy's side of the bed and scooped them up too, grabbing a pillow and dropping everything in as she hurried back through the bedroom. She ran down the hall, nearly stumbling on the steps as she rushed, and into the garage where Kathy was already behind the wheel. She darted into the passenger seat.

"A pillow? I don't need a–" Kathy started, alarmed, and looking around for the pill bottles.

"They're in there. Just drive!" Alice shouted, glancing back to see if Em was buckled in.

The garage door rolled up, and Kathy stomped on the gas. The noise must have alerted their intruders as two of them were standing there as the door opened, and Kathy sideswiped one.

"Oh, my God!" she gasped, alarmed.

"Don't stop!" Alice shouted, turning the wheel, and hearing the bump of the other man against the SUV. She looked around as the car faced

down the drive, and Kathy was putting it into drive. Several of their gardeners were fighting off men, and a couple of them were already down. Alice pressed a button, locking all the car doors at once.

Kathy stomped on the gas, and they all heard the squeal of the tires on the cobbled bricks of their expensive driveway. Several men looked up as she began to drive down the curved driveway. A couple broke away to cut her off. Kathy pressed the button on the visor to open the gate, not willing to wait for the gate to sense the car in the driveway.

Alice could hear shouting. Voices in Russian, Spanish, and English were yelling at them and at each other. Then, she heard the crash as Kathy ran into a car that suddenly appeared in front of them. They'd never seen it as they rushed down the drive. "Drive around it or through it!" Alice shouted.

Kathy tried. Her adrenaline was so high she was ready to take them all on. Her only thought was to get her wife and child away from these men. The crash slowed them enough that a man was able to smash the driver's window and slug her with a pistol. Everything stopped for her at that moment, especially when he slugged her again.

"Kathy!" Alice called, seeing how fast it had happened. She never saw the man coming to her passenger window, but suddenly, she was covered in glass. She looked up just as the butt of a rifle was heading towards her face. She turned, and it caught her on the side of her head. As she began to black out, she heard Emily's screams.

The End ~ for now ~ ☺ ~

If you have enjoyed **MACHIAVELLIAN MALICE**, I hope you
will enjoy this excerpt from

SHANGHAIED

Melissa Lawrence's life had been planned out for her. As a wife in the upper echelon of New York society, she was expected to take her place among some of the wealthiest people in America. A society that judges you on your looks will ignore certain things because of the money your family possesses, which you will eventually inherit; however, certain peccadillos will never be acceptable, and as Melissa becomes Mel and begins to realize her potential, life sends her on a journey she never could have anticipated.

CHAPTER ONE

As Mel began to come to, she listened to the sounds around her. She could hear shouts and conversations in several languages, clumping noises, metal grinding against metal, the creaking of wood, bangs, things rolling around, human sounds of snoring, farting, and breathing, squeaking of what she believed were rats, and above all that racket was the relentless sound of water. She could hear it faintly slapping against the thick wall her cheek was pressed tightly against. There were dreadful smells and something moist below her other cheek. It was a dampness and something else with an odor she couldn't identify. The wall was solid, a second sense told her that, but she could still identify the sound of water near her. Where was she?

"Get up! Get up!" a voice called, and she was suddenly sputtering as a bucketful of water splashed down on her barely awake and curiously numb face. Blinking rapidly, she could feel the sting of saltwater in her eyes. "Get yer arse up," a voice told her. Slowly, she

sat up from where she had been lying and tried to wipe the water from her eyes. Additional splashes of water hit her on both sides as buckets full of water were thrown on others around her. Blinking rapidly, she looked at the men lying about, some of them looking more confused than she. When one of the water bearers had all their attention, he said, "Yer on a ship at sea, and you'll be doing work, if you know what's good for ya. There hain't no way off 'er, and if you don't work, you don't eat. If you don't work, we'll throw ya overboard, and you'se can walk back!" He started to laugh at his own jest and the other two with him joined in.

Mel looked up at the man that was talking. He looked horrible. Bent over slightly, he snarled his words. He could have used a good shave and his clothes hadn't been cleaned…maybe ever. His face was in a permanent sneer, he was missing several teeth, and the teeth that remained were brown and fuzzy. His hands were gnarled looking. His shirt must have been white once, but now it was stained with dribble that had run down his scraggly beard and continued down the front of the material. His pantaloons were brown but faded from saltwater, and his scrawny but very hairy legs were darker from tanning and filth than his dirty pantaloons. He was barefooted, but the knives at his waist and a pistol held in a brightly colored red sash were well-worn and menacing, even if his countenance wasn't.

Standing behind that man were two others, one with a short whip in his dirty, hairy hands, the other wearing a patch over one eye with two pistols held in his hands and another two pistols wrapped in a bright orange sash at his waist. Neither man was taking any chances as they eyed their prisoners.

Mel looked around to see who he was talking to and saw four others sprawled on the filthy floor around her.

"Where are we?" one of the men laying beside Mel asked, reaching to hold his head.

"I tole yer," the man snarled. "Yer at sea, and I want ya up and workin' NOW!" he thundered.

"I need to be–" one man began but was struck down with a humiliating backhanded slap.

"I told ya where ya need to be," he snarled. "Get up and get ta work!" He leaned forward, grabbed the man by the neck of his shirt, and hurled him to the feet of his compatriots. The man behind him unfurled the short but deadly-looking whip.

Mel was one of the first to slowly rise, her height towering well above the gnarled man. It took a moment as she felt lightheaded; someone had obviously drugged her. The man eyed her warily and backed away slightly. He didn't know she was a woman, and why would he? She was big and built like an ox. Also, she had been wearing men's western wear and her hair was cut short, so there was no reason for them to suspect she wasn't a man. She knew better than to let on that she was anything other than what she appeared. She knew she was in a dangerous situation, much more dangerous than any of them realized. As a woman, she could easily be raped, and there would be no one to stop men like this. Furthermore, if they discovered the fortune she had on her person, her life would be agony until they no longer had a use for her, and then they would simply discard her into the sea. She didn't say a word. She knew the money she must have

had in her pockets was long gone. Her fine boots, her hat, and her leather jacket were also all gone.

A second man got up slowly. He too seemed to be intoxicated, the aftereffects of the drugs making him sluggish. "I don't think you understand. I can pay for–" he began, trying to sound reasonable.

The man smiled, baring his disgusting teeth. His fetid breath wafted across the distance separating him and the men he was standing over. "Anythin' you thought you had is ours. You gotta earn yer way across."

"But I assure you, I can–" the man said again, reaching for a wallet that wasn't there. "I've been robbed!" he gasped, incredulous at such an occurrence as he patted his pockets desperately. The three men standing over them laughed uproariously at his statement and chagrin.

Mel watched the man and the others, who were taking longer to come around. She could see one was just a boy. She glanced up as the man with the whip licked his lips, gazing at the boy and eying him up and down. She saw where he was looking.

"Yer gonna work yer way across," the man repeated, backhanding the man insultingly.

The man looked astounded to have been touched by the vulgar man and had started forward, intending to defend his honor, when the whip struck him. First, it hit his cheek, then his outstretched hand, and finally, his knee. Each crack of the whip echoed loudly in the small, enclosed area. Each strike landed a little harder, the third one causing his knees to buckle, and he went down, crying out at the pain. The three men seemed amused at his humiliation and obvious agony.

"Yer gonna have to learn to obey us," the man continued, thumb pointing at himself and his cronies.

Mel eyed them and then noticed the other two men and the boy slowly getting up, afraid not to. Fear was a motivating factor, and she saw them watching the three men warily. She waited to see what would happen next.

They were herded up top onto the heaving deck of the ship, falling against the walls of the stairwell, unsteady on their feet. Jeers, catcalls, and bawdy suggestions were yelled at them, especially the boy, and he flushed as he realized what they were suggesting. Mel could see he was afraid.

Each of them was assigned to a sailor, who would teach them what to do. Mel could see immediately that the sailors, who had the power of life or death over them, also didn't want to run afoul of those men who wielded the whip and gave the commands.

"Just do as yer told and you may get outta this alive," the older sailor she was assigned to told her helpfully.

Mel nodded, trying to clear the fogginess in her mind and glad that the numbness seemed to have subsided. She could see her companions were in varying degrees of shock over their sudden change in circumstances. One of them tried to argue and was whipped, kicked, and punched for his impunity. She saw the man, who had originally tried to argue, had learned his lesson as he limped painfully to do as he was told.

Many men were needed on a ship this size, and Mel looked around as she helped, using her immense strength to haul in lines the man gave her. There was no time to talk or exchange information but that didn't

mean it was quiet as the men continually shouted out to each other. She glanced up at the poop deck where a well-dressed man and several others stood. She assumed they were officers of the ship. She'd seen one of the new men rush up and try to reason with these better dressed gentlemen, only to be whipped and beaten for his temerity and then forced back to work.

"Not like that." The sailor teaching her showed her how to properly tie off the rope she was holding. "You want it to hold," he explained, sounding exasperated. When Mel got it wrong again, not seeing the twist he added to his tie, he backhanded her to discipline her. Mel stared at the man, making him distinctly uncomfortable as she waited silently for him to show her again. Once he had again demonstrated it, she duplicated the wrapping of the rope, realizing she had to tie it against itself, so it wouldn't come loose. That accomplished, they moved on to other things.

By midday, Mel was exhausted. The aftereffects of whatever knockout drug they had used on her had worn off. She was horribly thirsty and was relieved when the sailor approached a bucket and using a dipper, slurped up some of the water he pulled up. He offered it to Mel, and at first, the idea of drinking from the same vessel repulsed her, but looking about, she realized this was no time to be fastidious. She quickly drank, relieved to have her thirst assuaged, no matter how small the amount. They quickly went back to work. The cook and his helpers came around handing out bread, so the sailors didn't have to stop working. Mel was grateful to have something, anything in her stomach, but she worried as she had to use the necessary and knew there would be no facilities. The men peed at will, some over the sides,

and some squatting over a bucket, which they then threw over the side and washed out before towing it back with a rope for the next person. They didn't seem to mind if others saw them. Mel minded, especially seeing them make faces as they used the bucket. She would have to wait. She had no choice if she didn't want to be discovered. She had looked out over the water several times and saw no sign of land anywhere. San Francisco was long gone over the horizon.

Mel was a strong woman for the times, her hands used to hard work over the months and years she had herded cows. She used that strength to keep up with the spry, old sailor, who seemed to grunt out his satisfaction as she helped and learned the hard work. Having seen sailors effortlessly do such work for her in the past, she appreciated its difficulty now that she had to do it for them. She was watched all the time, from what she could tell. The others that had been shanghaied at the same time worked just as hard and were not fairing nearly as well. The other sailors smacked and even punched them into submission to get them to work. She worried over the boy but hadn't seen him since he had been assigned to one sailor, who looked innocent enough at first glance, but when she saw him up close, his eyes had radiated evil.

Mel realized this was far different from the pleasure cruises she and her father had taken between the Americas and Europe back in the day. These men didn't work for their passengers. There were no passengers that she could see, and there would be no staterooms or private bunks. These were the dregs of society, men she wouldn't have considered associating with at any time. They stayed out on their ships, working their lives away, then enjoying their times in port wenching, drinking, and gambling. The officers of the ship weren't much better, just better

dressed. A few of them even nattily dressed after having just come from port. The shanghaied men were treated as mere slaves, along with a few others, who hadn't dared to desert the horrible ship. Mel kept her head down, did as she was told, and tried to learn.

Dinner was a watery fish stew with more bread. Mel was disgusted to find weevils in the bread, but she used her nail to flick the wiggling critters out of her food, inspecting it closely each time before she took a bite, so she wouldn't accidentally eat one of the disgusting, wriggling creatures. She tried not to be too fastidious as it would give her away. Her nails and hands were filthy, as were those around her also joggling for space on the table as the ship rocked and rolled over the water. Everything that wasn't nailed down on their table rolled around on its flat surface. Slurping, belching, and farting their way through the meal, many just wiped their lips and moustaches on their sleeves and shirts. Mel followed suit, knowing the more she fit in, the less they would notice her.

"Yer a strong one," someone commented, and Mel nodded, not wishing to engage in conversation and give herself away. She affected a lower voice, something she had used before when people assumed she was a man. It wasn't difficult, her naturally melodic voice lower than most women. After finishing her meal, the sailor she had been assigned to, Humphrey Duggins, showed her where she could bunk in a hammock slung between two pillars of the ship along with forty other men. No one was sleeping this early. Several were playing cards, a couple were drinking, and the lights were low, so there was no worry about fire. Others were going about the ship on their own business,

some staying up top to work and watch in case they were needed, and others were just enjoying the cold night air.

Mel examined her new accommodations, worrying about her full bladder and wondering how she could get a moment alone to empty it. Also, dinner hadn't set well with her, and she worried that it would loosen her bowels. She knew some of it was the trepidation she was feeling and genuine fear over this dangerous situation.

Left alone, she made her way back towards the cargo hold, making it look like she was heading up onto the deck for air. She slipped behind some casks with a bucket she had grabbed, knowing from its smell it had already been used for the same purpose she was about to use it for. She had a hard time seeing and hoped no one would come upon her. She bent over, quickly pulling down her trousers and slipping aside the men's summer underwear she had been wearing, so she could make her stream. She slipped aside the two rolls of coins she had hidden there, awkwardly having learnt to walk despite them. She tried not to think about them as she squatted, relieving first her bladder and then quickly, her bowels. The odor rose in the enclosed space, and she heard others in the hold. The rhythmic sounds told her what they were about as they used each other on this male-only ship. She only hoped they didn't hear the noises she made into the bucket as she quickly finished up, disgusted that she didn't have a paper to wipe her backside. Resigned to her situation, she quickly pulled up her trousers and took the bucket topside to throw it overboard, being careful to stay out of the wind, so it wouldn't come back on board or splash her person. Having just learned how to tie a proper knot that day, she was

pleased with herself for tying the rope on the handle, so she could throw it overboard and wash out the bucket.

"Ya did good today," a voice said as she finished cleaning the bucket and went to return it to the hold. She hadn't seen the man smoking the pipe in the dark and this disturbed her, almost as though she had been caught out.

"Thank ye," she responded, figuring that keeping her answers short and sweet would be her best bet under the circumstances. She continued toward the hold, going down the nearly vertical steps and making her way to her hammock after she put the bucket down by the door.

"'Bout time you got back with that," someone groused as he loosened his trousers and squatted without any fanfare, not caring that he was exposed to everyone else in the area.

Mel hurried away from the disagreeable man, not wishing to be around him or his disgusting habits. Still, she figured it must be the norm as no one else seemed to notice or care. She saw one of her fellow shipmates that had been shanghaied with her, and he was sporting a black eye. She turned away, unable to help him and hoping he would fare better tomorrow. Climbing into her hammock took some doing, and she was alarmed when another man came over and climbed into the hammock above her. His ass was right above her, and knowing the men's habits already, she knew she couldn't escape the noxious odors that would likely escape from him. She pulled up her blanket, nearly burying her face in it and welcoming the warmth when it trapped her body heat and she began to warm. She didn't sleep soundly. Too

many men came and went, and she was nervous about sleeping too deeply and having anyone find her out.

She'd been told she would be roused for her shift, and after four hours she heard some of the others moving about. She rose before they could wake her and used the bucket again. Carrying it to her hiding place, she was quick, having waited until her body was nearly bursting. She cleaned it out because no one else seemed to care, then replaced it and headed to breakfast with the others.

To be continued……

Check out all my books at: www.kannemeinel.com.

About the Author

K'Anne Meinel is a Lesbian Fiction bestselling author with more than 100 published works including shorts, novellas, and novels. She is an American author born in Milwaukee, Wisconsin and raised in Oconomowoc. Upon early graduation from high school she went to a private college in Milwaukee and then moved to California for seventeen years before returning to the state. Many of her stories have Wisconsin in them as settings for her wonderful, realistic, and detailed backgrounds. Named the lesbian Danielle Steel of her time, K'Anne continues to write interesting stories in a variety of genres in both the lesbian and mainstream fiction categories.

~ Because a publisher should stand behind their authors~

What do you do when you meet someone who changes everything you know about love and passion?

Paige Harlow is a good girl. She's always known where she was going in life: top grades, an ivy league school, a medical degree, regular church attendance, and a happy marriage to a man. So falling in love with her gorgeous roommate and best friend Alyssa Torres is no small crisis. Alyssa is chasing demons of her own, a medical condition that makes her an outcast and a family dysfunctional to the point of disintegration make her a questionable choice for any stable relationship. But Paige's heart is no longer her own. She must now battle the prejudices of her family, friends, and church and come to peace with her new sexuality before she can hope to win the affections of the woman of her dreams. But will love be enough?

~ Because a publisher should stand behind their authors~

When Delaney Delacroix is called to locate a missing girl, she never plans on getting caught up with a human trafficking investigation or with the local witch. Meeting with Raelin Montrose changes her life in so many ways that Delaney isn't sure that this isn't destiny.

Raelin Montrose is a practicing Wiccan, and when the ley lines that run under her home tell her that someone is coming, she can't imagine that she was going to solve a mystery and find the love of her life at the same time.

~ Because a publisher should stand behind their authors~

Amelia Gittens had the credit of being the first and only woman thus far in the United States military of being a sniper in combat, made possible by being in the Military Police unit of the crack 10th Mountain Infantry Division. After retirement she joins the City of New York Police Department, and suddenly finds herself involved in a suspect shooting incident which soon encroaches upon her entire life. In order to protect her therapist who has been targeted as a revenge killing, Amelia takes on the responsibility as if she was still in the Army, treating it as a tactical maneuver.

An abused and bullied teenager is suddenly granted great and terrible powers by an ancient goddess. Each step towards womanhood is shaped by her new abilities, as is the woman she will become. Devil or angel, which will she be? Will the woman who chases her ever know for sure?

Both men tried to shoot her then, and the two women were stunned at the speed with which she moved. Penny charged straight at the gunmen then dove under their fire. Spinning on her back she kicked the legs from under one man, and as he fell, she kicked the gun from the other man's hand. Spinning back to the first man she saw the gun barrel moving toward her, and she lashed out with her foot. Her boot crushed his skull and she rolled to her feet to grab the last man in a neck lock. A quick twist and he lay lifeless in her arms.

She let him fall, as, breathing deeply, she came down off combat mode. "Are you ladies all right?" she asked as she untied the ropes that held the older woman.

"Who are you?" asked the old woman fearfully, as she pulled the tape from her mouth.

"They call me Lady Blue," smiled Penny as she helped the woman to stand.

"What are you?" It was the younger woman who spoke.

"Cold, hungry, dead tired, and covered in blue war paint," giggled Penny as she released the older woman's arm. She turned and began to search the bodies.

*If you have enjoyed this book and the others listed here Shadoe
Publishing is always looking for first, second, or third time
authors. Please check out our website @
www.shadoepublishing.com
For information or to contact us @
shadoepublishing@gmail.com.*

*We may be able to help you make your dreams of becoming
a published author come true.*

www.ingramcontent.com/pod-product-compliance
Lightning Source LLC
Chambersburg PA
CBHW070758120626
46557CB00002B/657